UNCLE VINCENT'S HOUSE

STEVEN BEAI

This one is for Julian, Kaden and Rayven.
Always together, forever friends.

PART ONE

Harris, Indiana

Chapter One

Allegiance and Traditions

The Little Italy Festival is something I've looked forward to every year since the second grade.

I remember the week leading up to Labor Day Weekend when Mrs. Stringfellow would regale us with stories about the holiday. Specifically, what Labor Day meant to our town of Harris, Indiana.

Immigrants from every corner of Italy migrated to the United States from Ellis Island and somehow found their way *en masse* over two thousand miles away from the towering Lady Liberty to the squat little town of Harris on the banks of the Wabash River.

Mrs. Stringfellow looked across the class in her calm manner, a faint smile on her face as she spoke. "Many of our ancestors decided to move inland to seek work in places reminding them of their homeland villages rather than settle in New York. Even at that time, New York was overcrowded and so they came here to make their living in the coal mines."

That day, returning from lunch, we all entered the classroom to find Mrs. Stringfellow was not there. I glanced around and not seeing her, blurted out prematurely.

"We're in luck!"

Instantly, Mrs. Stringfellow stepped out from the open doorway of the coat closet, firing an accusing index finger in my direction.

"No, you're NOT in luck!" she snapped.

My face suddenly felt white-hot and I lowered my eyes as we took our seats. Nothing more was said of the incident, but I was filled with embarrassment and anxiety. Only years later did I realize what I had felt was shame. I had hurt her feelings with my offhand comment implying that she was somehow bad. A bully. A tyrant because of her authority, which I'd never thought was the case. Although proper to the point of seeming aloof, Mrs. Stringfellow was my favorite teacher.

"How many of you have family who worked the coal mines?"

All but a few in our class thrust eager arms into the air. Chastened by Mrs. Stringfellow's dress-down, I kept my arms on the desk. For me, it was my Grandpa Deno, Mom's dad, who had died before I was born. Dad told me stories about him, though, stories about how his father-in-law had worked the filthy and thankless Black Diamond mine to provide a good life for his family. I was a part of this classroom conversation, worthy of raising my hand, but fearful of any more attention, good or bad, so I remained still while Mrs. Stringfellow continued.

"No matter what your families did, or where they came from, *all* of us are an important part of our town. Just by calling Harris our home, we honor its legacy and those who came before."

"We're all Americans!" I shouted impulsively. My voice rang out over the silence of the classroom. Instantly, my face burned red-hot. I sank down against the wooden back of my chair. My stomach churned. Again, I was exposed, alone, with only myself to blame.

"That's right!" Mrs. Stringfellow yelled, pointing that same accusing finger in my direction now as a validation. She gave me a maternal wink.

"That's what we are, Julian Baker, very nicely said!"

I straightened into my chair, redeemed. Mrs. Stringfellow didn't hate me after all. A circus of confusing concepts played inside my head. A calliope filled with judgments and grudges, of conflict and forgiveness and all manner of life lessons too complicated for me to grasp. Lessons that wouldn't coalesce for many years. There was so much more to learn.

Her eyes moved over the class and across the windows before settling on the flaccid piece of cloth hanging from a tarnished silver pole to her right.

Mrs. Stringfellow raised her arms to the ceiling, urging us to rise.

"Let's all stand and pledge allegiance to our flag," she said.

And so, we did, standing stiffly, our right hands glued to our chests as we stared at the curled, unmoving flag and recited the pledge in unison without understanding what the words truly meant.

Chapter Two

Festival Weekend

I was going after a salami.

"I'm gettin' that cheese wheel!" Rayven said, thrusting his hands into both pockets of his jeans and coming out with two handfuls of dimes. He smiled into his palms. "*Shitfire*, maybe I'll win a cheese wheel *and* a salami!" He rattled the change in his fists before thrusting them back into his pockets, grinning at me like a lunatic. He slapped me on the back, hard. "Yeah, man, let's *GO!*"

Rayven was big for his age, had always seemed adult-sized since I could remember. As we made our way to our favorite attraction, I marveled at the fact that we were both fifteen, yet my eyes only reached his chin. Rayven wore a perpetual grin and laughed in endless frequent bursts, no matter the situation, forever good-natured.

His mother, my Aunt Laurie, was like Rayven; always cheerful and full of life, always looking on the bright side of things. She'd wrapped Dad in her arms at my mother's funeral while they both cried. Both she and Uncle Vincent comforted Dad, assuring him they would get through Mom's death together. Vincent whispered a tearful guarantee in Dad's ear that everything would be okay. His thin arm reached down to tousle the hair of the toddler attached to his brother's leg. *Me.* His little nephew he loved as much as his own three children. So I've been told anyway. I don't remember any of it. Especially the part where Vincent Baker comforted anyone.

From my earliest memories, Uncle Vincent was an imposing figure. He never smiled and always seemed to be looming over me, devoid of any kind of emotion, like a scarecrow. Rayven never noticed my discomfort and spoke of him in glowing terms. Dad never spoke to me about him at all but I could tell he was fond of his brother. I was the only one scared of Uncle Vincent and would avoid him whenever he visited our house by himself. Dad would make excuses for me throughout my grade school years. During that time, my world consisted of only me and my father.

Until the fifth grade when I shared classes with my cousin Rayven. We became fast friends in school and were excited when we would meet on holidays like Halloween, Christmas, Memorial Day, and birthdays. Labor Day weekends exploring the Little Italy Festival together became a tradition.

Now, as Seniors in our final high-school year, we stalked through the festival grounds like two warriors looking for adventure over the long weekend.

Boasting a population of just under five thousand people, Harris swelled to the seams every Labor Day Weekend. The Little Italy Festival drew thousands more attendees from all over Indiana and surrounding States, tripling the population and then some.

There were dozens of craft booths and food kiosks. Live music was everywhere; near the Four Seasons Fountain overlooking the Wabash River, on the banks of the river below and all through the town. The tractor ride was an omnipresent feature for festivalgoers, the transportation to every main event: The Wine Gardens, where adults would celebrate late into the night. The Black Diamond Coal Museum, twenty feet from the railroad tracks cutting through the town. The museum was housed in what had been Harris' train depot years before I was born. I was told stories of my grandparents waiting on the platform to catch the train to vacation in Chicago. Now, locomotives blew past the building at full speed with a deafening roar, quickly leaving Harris behind. To me, the curious building had always been the Black Diamond Coal Mine Museum.

The tractor ran from one end of town to the other. For 75 cents, both joyriders and tired citizens calling it a night could sit on two long wagons fitted with bleacher seats pulled by one of three green John Deere tractors piloted by local farmers to go from Main Street to the Wine Gardens or for a shorter walk home and to bed. As the tractors roared through town, all riders would wave and scream at the people on the streets and those on foot would holler back with the same revelry. Whether on the tractor or walking the sidewalks of Harris as it passed, happy shouts and echoes of greetings was an honored festival tradition. The tractor ride was a long-standing revered ritual, an almost holy experience in the secular world of the festival. But it couldn't compare to the Lions Club booth and its roulette wheel promise of winning a roll of fresh salami or succulent wheel of local cheese.

We pushed through madding crowds of shuffling people, Rayven leading the way. He darted and zig-zagged through families and loose, staring groups. Nudging drunk and shuffling people out of his way, Rayven cleared our path to the Lions Club booth. The square-roofed tent stood out like a beacon in a thunderstorm. Suddenly, the noise of the crowd dimmed, the live music blaring from every direction lost its treble and both coalesced into a dull background hum.

The booth was surrounded by people on the three sides open to the public, all of them laughing and yelling and fidgeting in place as they slapped their dimes down on the narrow counter before them. Each of the three counters were bordered with painted squares. Inside each square was a number corresponding to the prize-wheel in the booth.

Three counters surrounded by at least sixty people.

Two ways to win.

First, you could lay down your dime on a number and that number might come up yellow on the wheel. Hitting on yellow multiplied your bet times ten, turning a dime into a dollar.

Second, and most desired, was hitting on a red number. Hitting on red meant your choice of a two-foot-long salami roll or a three-pound cheese wheel.

The wheel itself had both yellow and red of all thirty numbers. A member of the Lions Club, generally a senior member, both rolled the wheel and manned the microphone, while other members watched the three counters, monitoring the bets for any sign of cheating and verifying any wins.

The senior Lions Club member urged the people into a dime-betting frenzy:

"Okay, folks, here we go again! Cheese or salami, salami or cheese, place your bets! Place your bets! Win a cheese or salami, your choice! Salami or cheese made fresh right here in Harris, c'mon, folks, lay those bets down! Lay 'em down!"

As the wheel spun round and round, the patter continued until the wheel began to wind down:

"No more bets! No more bets! Have your money down! No more bets please! Cheese or salami, what'll it be?!"

The metal tang gave a final *click* against a steel peg as the wheel stopped.

"Twenty-two yellow! YELLOW twenty-two! A dollar for a dime!"

Over the cacophony of voices from the crowd making their way down the long street above the Wabash River, the collective groan was heard for a quarter mile in every direction, from the Vermillion Beverage building on Chestnut Street up to Main Street, a block away. Even the ticket-seller for the tractor ride inside his narrow plywood booth at the far end of Main Street heard it and blurted out *Oh, no!* or *Winner! Salami or cheese!* in between selling tickets. "Don't forget to visit the Lions Club booth, folks!" he added every now and then. "Try your luck for a dime and win a cheese or salami!"

Every year it was the same. The opening parade on Friday afternoon snaking from Bogart Street at one end of town to Main Street on the opposite end of Harris at the Wabash bridge.

The crowds. The booths. The music and the electricity of a small town coming together for seventy-two hours as a single entity. A three-day party. Holding it all together was the ethereal backbeat of the frustrated groans and celebratory shouts from a small booth in the center of it all where people gambled a dime to win a salami or cheese, their shouts rising above the town to create its own atmosphere at a single point in time in the sky high above an otherwise insignificant town.

Each Labor Day weekend, for almost three days, it seemed anything was possible.

Rayven grabbed a handful of my Batman t-shirt just above Adam West's head, tugging me behind as he pushed his way between two people, sidling up to the booth. He pressed his stomach against the counter and slapped down three dimes; one on number twenty-one, one on seven and one on fifteen as I looked over his shoulder.

"No more bets!"

Click-clack went the wheel, clattering to a stop.

"Seven yellow! Seven Yellow! Pays ten-to-one!"

The Lions Club attendant at our counter raised a hand.

"Seven Yellow here! We got a winner folks!"

The attendant cleared the board, leaving Rayven's single dime on Number Seven and counting out nine more dimes in the square.

Rayven scooped up the coins and pulled me alongside him. He deposited the ten dimes in my hand, yelling in my ear "Let's go for it! *Let's cover the board!*"

There were thirty number possibilities. It cost three dollars to place a dime on every number. Even though you were guaranteed to "win" by covering the board, if whatever number came up yellow, you ended up losing two bucks.

I scattered my dimes to the right, covering numbers twenty-one through thirty.

Rayven had twenty dimes left and covered the numbers one through twenty.

The wheel started to spin.

I looked over the board from left to right at the scattered dimes on every number.

Two dimes sat on Number Seventeen. Rayven's and someone else's. I stared at the number seventeen square for what seemed an eternity, listening to the wheel clatter to its result.

"Okay, folks...."

An instant before the wheel slowed, before the words *no more bets* echoed over the crowd, I moved my dime from number twenty-one to Rayven's dime on seventeen, leaving number twenty-one vacant. Three dimes on Number Seventeen. Rayven's. Mine. Someone else's.

"Seventeen Red! *Red seventeen! Three* Winners, folks! Cheese or salami! *Three winners!*"

Hysterical shouts rose from the booth, rattling over the crowd into the sky above. Up on Main Street, the ticket-seller at the tractor booth cocked his head to listen as his customers froze.

Rayven and I locked our eyes, mouths agape.

"*Salami!*" a voice yelled.

Another voice yelled "*Cheese!*" and I knew at once it was Rayven.

"*Salami!*" I countered, blurting out my choice before I could think about what had just happened.

The Lions Club volunteer slapped a salami down on the counter in front of the first winner who held it above his head and *whooped* to the crowd. Then, a cheese wheel in front of Rayven, followed quickly by a roll of salami for me.

"*Three winners on red, folks!* Lay down a dime and win a cheese or salami!"

We backed away from the counter, holding our bounty and laughing to beat the band. A wheel of cheese *and* a roll of salami! For just three measly bucks! How lucky could we get?! *We won! Both of us!!*

The frenzy of the crowd exploded as news of the triple-win on red spread over the other two sides of the booth and into passers-by on the street. As we retreated from our spots at the counter clutching our bounty tightly to our chests, I lost count of how many times I was jostled around by smiling faces. Rayven was grinning from ear to ear, returning every congratulatory pat on the back with a raucous cheer followed by booming laughter, like some lusty barbarian returning victorious from a hard-won conquest. I kept my head down as I made my way from the booth, mumbling quiet *thank-yous*. For a heartbeat or two, I felt like a celebrity.

The final pat on my back came from Rayven, hearty and painful, causing me to momentarily lose balance. I smiled despite my stumble.

Suddenly, Rayven's arm was around my neck, pulling us shoulder to shoulder.

"*Sonofabitch, man!* Can you believe that? *Wotta win!*"

I inhaled deeper than I thought possible, searching for words. "I...I...maaan..."

He rattled me without letting up. "Yeah, *um, um,*" he mocked. "Mr. Humble! If you hadn't moved that dime like you did...it was *you*, Julian! A Triple-Red! Holy Tap-Dancing Christ!" Rayven released his hold on me and took his cheese wheel in both hands, holding it up to the sky.

"Cheese Wheel!" he shouted. Lowering his arms, he planted a kiss on the cheese.

"A salami!" I shouted in response. I planted a kiss on my bounty. "We'll eat like Kings!"

Behind us, the Lion's Club booth was swarming five-deep on all three sides with people gambling and those waiting to gamble their dimes on another triple-win. All I could see of the booth now was the yellow canopy swaying in the gentle breeze.

The sound of the roulette wheel's *clack-clack-clack* faded as we made our way down Water Street.

We stopped at the Four Seasons Fountain, overlooking the Wabash River. More booths and attractions littered the riverbank; food kiosks and competing band shells on opposite ends of the bank. At the single concrete launch sat the ornate hut selling tickets for the Gondola ride on the river. A half-dozen Gondolas floated over slow-rolling currents as Hoosiers experienced the imported Italian thrill. A few years later, three people would drown after one of the Gondolas capsized in the wide and powerful water and that was that. The insurance liability was out of reach for the town and the Gondola rides faded into Festival history. But now, in that moment, we listened to the disjointed echoes of "O! Sole Mio" sung by six different Gondola pilots rise into the air above the water as we sat on the edge of the fountain, marveling at our prizes without a word.

The glow of our victory was fading fast. I felt the ebbing triumph slowly changing back to the ordinary as sure as my fingers felt the stiff coldness of the tightly wrapped salami roll in my hands. Behind us, the energy of the Triple-Red win still pulsed around the Lion's Club booth, but we were no longer a part of it. I could tell Rayven felt it, too. Turning my head to gaze up Elm Street, I had an epiphany.

"Tractor ride." I said.

Rayven hopped off the edge of the fountain. "You bet!"

We hurried up Elm Street, running past the plate glass windows of Mike's Motors Chrysler dealership, and took a hard right onto Main in front of the booth selling tickets for the tractor ride. As we caught our breath, we were greeted by a group of our classmates already in line for tickets. Smiling, I waved at them.

"Hey, Bakers!" David Sills yelled from the group. Seeing our cheese and salami, his face grew beatific. His red hair looked almost like a head wound above the pale skin of his face. "Hey, you guys won big, praise God."

"Hey, David," I said as Rayven grinned down at his cheese wheel, then back at David with a bright *Yeah*.

Roger Gallo appeared, wearing his usual sleeveless T-shirt and crusty jeans. He yanked David close and said something into David's ear I couldn't hear. David's smile disappeared. He tried to pull away, but Roger held him fast. I heard him snarl "You little Jesus Freak."

David tried to push him away. "Get off me."

Gallo pushed him out of line with a booming laugh. A couple of other guys in our group joined in the laughter.

Rayven stepped forward, calling out to our classmate. "What's so funny, Bill?" He came up to Bill Purcell. "How about I knock your dick in the dirt? Think that'd be funny?" Instantly, Bill Purcell stared at his shoes.

Rayven turned to Roger Gallo and took a step to him, nose to nose. "Leave him alone. Or fuck around and find out."

Roger Gallo looked like he might throw up right then and there. He raised his palms to Rayven. "Hey, it's cool, man."

The rest of the group piled on Roger and Bill, lightly cuffing their shoulders. "Don't be an asshole," one of the guys said.

"For Gallo, that's a birth defect," I said loudly.

13

David's eyes flashed a moist look of gratitude at us. He turned to look over our friends. "C'mon, guys, it's the tractor ride, let's all just have a good time."

"Save us a couple of seats up top," Rayven called as we went to the back of the line.

In fifth grade, Rayven had spent the night at David Sills' house, arriving there on a Friday shortly after school. Friday and Saturday sleepovers were big deals for everyone back then. It was a given that you could stay up late and watch scary movies or play games outside after it got dark. Maybe you could even pitch a pup tent and camp out in the back yard. One never knew what their friend's parents had planned, but parents hosting the sleepovers always had something special prepared. And among us all, Rayven Baker was considered the Sleepover King, having spent almost as much time at the homes of his friends as he did his own.

During his one and only sleepover at David's things were different. The Sills family was deeply religious. The phrase "to a fault" comes to mind.

The sun had barely set on that late Spring Friday afternoon, before Rayven had had time to contemplate the fun of spending the night at a friend's house; the night had ended abruptly before it ever began. At seven o' clock, Rayven had found himself in a basement twin bed next to David's twin bed. Time to go to sleep. For the next five hours, David had poured out his life to Rayven, speaking in furtive, whispered detail with almost apologetic embarrassment about how he and his younger brothers and sisters lived. Staying up until seven o' clock was allowed on Friday and Saturday nights only. Every other day of the week, bedtime was at six o' clock. David had explained that sleeping in the basement was considered a *special treat* by his parents. Rayven never knew exactly what religious denomination the Sills Family cleaved to. David never did say, except to say that they were *very* religious. Rayven would throw out favorite bands like Van Halen, favorite movies like *Curse of Frankenstein* or TV shows like *The Twilight Zone* re-runs. David had never heard of any of them, completely unaware of their mere existence. Rayven was awestruck. Just the same, David was a good guy.

He was sincere and honest. Although he would never spend another night at David's house, Rayven liked him.

The next Monday at school, Rayven had related his overnight experience with David to several friends. He'd tried to explain the strange religious proclivities of David's parents without making David himself seem culpable, but he missed the mark. David Sills became the victim of choice not only for bullies, but many classmates as well. That this sudden hazing of someone he liked was his fault weighed on Rayven until the guilt he carried became a sword he bore gladly from the fifth grade to high school. Although he and David had never gotten closer than that sleepover, Rayven always came to his defense.

Tickets in hand, we clambered up the wooden steps to our waiting seats on top of the wagon. Rayven sidled down next to Roger Gallo, tucking his cheese wheel under his arm. He laid his free hand on Gallo's thigh and I could see the fingers close over his jeans. Gallo's eyes went wide in pain. Rayven jerked his thigh this way and that, too slight for anyone else to notice. Rayven leaned into Gallo's left ear.

"No more with David, okay? Not ever again."

Rayven clenched tighter and Gallo winced, eyes squeezing shut in pain.

"*Never* again."

Gallo trembled. "I got it."

The tractor rumbled over the streets tugging its human cargo behind on two connected wagons that coughed at every turn and jerked with each new acceleration. Lording over one wagon, the boys sat straight-backed on the top two bleacher seats, waving and screaming at the sidewalks filled with other festivalgoers walking in opposite directions on either side of the street. Some were heading for the fairgrounds toward the river; others heading uptown toward the Wine Garden and other attractions.

Most of the walkers carried six or twelve-packs of beer. Some carried single bottles of beer they pulled from as they made their way to hidden destinations. All were drunk, either from the free-flowing alcohol, festival reverie, or both. They shouted and waved back with occasional applause as the John Deere tractors roared past. At certain points, two tractors would meet going separate directions and the wagons of both erupted in cheers. The prevailing atmosphere over Harris during Labor Day Weekend, during the Little Italy Festival was pure jubilation. Pure freedom without anarchy or anger. The local bars were filled, yet no fights ever broke out, no gunshots were ever heard, no arrests ever made. There were out-of-town bikers glowering behind bearded faces as they slowly cruised the streets on roaring Harleys proudly wearing their sleeveless vests adorned with club patches and crimson skulls. There were young families with small children in tow, taking in the festival on foot. There were Harris Police Officers moving down the streets in patrol cars and on foot. They all would wave at one another, smile a greeting, or offer a hand to some out-of-towner who wanted directions to the Coal Town Museum. Once a year, in this corner of the world, in this town, it was beyond idyllic.

It was perfect.

The tractor stopped alongside the carwash on Blackman Street before heading down Ninth Street and to the Wine Garden.

The sun glowed a bright yellow on the horizon, still a few hours from twilight.

David Sills stood up. "Here I am, guys. Gotta go."

Roger Gallo left his seat, held out a hand. "See ya later. Tomorrow maybe?"

"Sure thing," David smiled.

Gallo looked down at Rayven, who nodded. Exhaling, Gallo sat back down, relief washing over his face. Rayven patted his knee and Gallo's shoulder butted against Rayven's shoulder as if to say he was sorry.

David jumped from the wagon to the sidewalk. He started to walk away and looked back, making eye contact with me.

"Bless you guys," he said.

"You, too, Dave," I said. "Thanks."

He nodded. "See you!"

I watched him walk down the sidewalk as the tractor pulled away, his back squared, his footsteps sure and steady as he made his way back home.

Overhead, the sun dimmed into twilight as night approached. The festival lights over Harris shone brighter, the music became more raucous. The whole of the town seemed to adjust its collective personality in response to the darkness, as if to sustain the light in spirit if not literal.

"Shitfire," Rayven said as we disembarked from the tractor in front of the Wine Garden.

"Saves matches," I said automatically.

In front of me, Rayven was on the sidewalk at the Wine Garden entrance, looking up at the sky. Beyond the open doors of the Wine Garden, draped with plastic grapes and Italian flags, indistinct voices and loud music mingled together from the tables and stage on the banks of Feather Creek. Suddenly, I heard the opening strains of Steely Dan's "Reelin' in the Years" and the distinct drumming of my dad. I imagined him sitting behind the desert burst Tama kit covered in beads of sweat as he pounded out the song's rhythm.

I grabbed Rayven's arm. "What's wrong?"

"I can't get home now. It's too late. Shitfire if I can remember whether Mom and Dad said they were coming in town tonight or tomorrow for the festival. I was supposed to watch Cami and Evie when they came into town. I was supposed to be home with them for the night."

I tried to counter the panic on Rayven's face, the agitation that appeared at once over his entire body in the form of his increasing fidgeting over the sidewalk.

All I could muster was the word "Tonight?"

Rayven stomped the sidewalk, fists clenching.

"I can't remember!"

Cami and Evie were fifteen years old, a minuscule eighteen months behind our age. I couldn't understand why Rayven was filled with such panic at the thought of his sisters being at home by themselves, whether Uncle Vincent and Aunt Laurie were there or not.

"It's not like they're gonna burn the house down," I tried.

17

"Julian!" Rayven barked, taking me by the shoulders. "You don't understand! My sisters are *my* responsibility when my folks are gone, I have to make sure that nothing happens—"

A booming voice cut him off, yelling our names. Seconds later, long arms encircled Rayven's neck and pulled him backwards.

It was Uncle Vincent, emerging from the Wine Garden. He scowled at me, looking mean as ever.

Chapter Three

Casey Woodruff

"What're you delinquents doing here?!"

Uncle Vincent had always reminded me of the butler in every haunted house movie I'd ever seen. Tall and thin with short black hair parted on the side like someone from a hundred years ago. His face was gaunt with dark eyes, somehow...*hypnotic*. I guess girls would describe it as handsome. He was dressed like everyone else on the street: blue jeans and a T-shirt with the name of a college across the chest. Michigan State maybe. I couldn't remember ever seeing him smile or hearing him laugh.

My dad, on the other hand, sported long hair, sideburns, and usually a three-day stubble. He was quick to laugh, not so buttoned-up as Uncle Vincent. People were always shocked to find out they were brothers and close ones, at that.

When Rayven talked about his father, it was always in general terms, like going fishing or to the Indianapolis 500, casual stories he related fondly. Still, there was a secretive aspect to his father that, if Rayven knew, he kept to himself. Still holding fast to Rayven, Uncle Vincent's eyes burned into mine.

"Hear your dad in there?"

Inside the Wine Garden, The Strays were playing a Blue Oyster Cult cover, "Godzilla." The bass and drums pulsed out into the street.

I swallowed hard and managed to say, "Sounds good."

Rayven looked close to having a full-blown fit of panic. Was Vincent about to release some sort of unholy wrath on both of us because Cami and Evie had been abandoned by Rayven?

"Damn right, he sounds good." He released Rayven. "The Garden's packed full." Seeing the cheese wheel and salami we were holding; Uncle Vincent aimed his index finger at us. "A good weekend all around."

Before Rayven could speak, Vincent continued.

"Listen, your mom and I are gonna close out the Garden, stay for the whole show. John said you can spend the night with Julian at their house. We'll probably be rolling in there later, but don't you guys stay out too late. Your sisters are staying at the Woodruff's with their friend tonight and tomorrow—*but you know that already from the note we left.* Anyway, you guys be good."

Before he turned to go back inside, Vincent lit a cigarette, taking a deep drag and exhaling a thick rope of smoke into the humid night air. The three of us watched it expand slowly as it rose into the darkness.

"Good timing," Vincent said after the ascending white cloud had dissipated. He looked back down at us. "Came out here for a smoke and here you are. I'll tell Mom I saw you, son. Your Dad, too, Julian."

"Thanks, uncle."

Vincent tipped his cigarette to me in response before taking another drag. He gave Rayven a hug with his free arm.

"If you boys are gonna stay out for much longer you might want to stop by Julian's house and put that stuff in the refrigerator."

"We will, Dad," Rayven answered. "Thanks."

"Love you, son."

"Love you, too, Dad."

We were two blocks away from the Wine Garden, the sound of the music reduced to fading booms from the bass drum, when I declared with deadpan certainty "You didn't see the note."

Rayven shook his head with relief.

"No, I did not."

"*Shitfire.*"

Cami and Evie Baker were not identical twins but the other kind, fraternal I think it's called. Cami had her mom's rosy features and blonde hair while Evie was rail-thin with her father's dark hair and perpetually distant look. They were good students, like their brother, while I considered myself average or maybe a little above, earning my share of "C" grades as they did "As" and "Bs". Beyond good-natured ribbings, Rayven and his sisters never outright fought the typical raging life-and-death battles so common to siblings of any age. Having just my only-child self in comparison, the lack of enmity seemed normal. Uncle Vincent, Aunt Laurie, Rayven, Cami, and Evie were a family and families stuck together. Just like me and Dad.

On the other hand, was the freak of nature known as Casey Woodruff, best friend to the twins. And the twins, as far as I knew, were Creepy Casey's *only* friends.

If Uncle Vincent came across as a little dark and stoic, Casey Woodruff was *stygian*. She was lean, almost skeletal, which made her seem taller than she was. Her skin was pale to the point of cadaverous, almost as white as notebook paper. Wide black eyes bordered a delicate nose leading to full red lips which didn't seem to fit her face. Framing it all was impossibly straight jet-black hair running down to the middle of her back. Razor-sharp bangs covered her forehead, not quite touching her thin, intense eyebrows. She wore black eye shadow and dark clothes exclusively. A *Goth Girl* one might assume at first glance, but for Casey Woodruff it was no costume or fashion statement. The girl was truly haunted, I thought, albeit in an intriguing way I resisted admitting to myself. She was like a stray animal the twins had adopted.

Rayven ignored her with ease when she was around but I always found myself stealing glances at her, never understanding why. Was my curiosity that of a spectator attending a midway freak-show? A rubberneck at a final violent traffic accident? Or something else? Something in the way Creepy Casey seemed to float when she moved, slowly and deliberately, her arms and legs in unison with every move she made. Walking. Standing. Sitting cross-legged in a circle with Cami and Evie as they commanded their self-constructed world of Barbie dolls or played board games, she stood out no matter what the setting, as if illuminated by a ghost-light shining down from everywhere and nowhere. In the last few months, I'd had a handful of dreams disguised as nightmares where Casey was present. The dreams were always the same: I was in a house of horrors, looking out from a tower window down at the town of Harris, far below. Suddenly, a cold chill blew over me and I turned to see Casey Woodruff floating over the floor, hands outstretched as she came forward for me, her eyes glistening pools of solid white. She took me in her arms, raising my body until we were eye to eye. My hair stood on end as I waited to be enveloped by the pure essence of eternal evil. I closed my eyes and the chill turned to the warmth of a comforter over a welcoming bed. I felt her lips press into mine, moist and full, her slender arms wrapped around my back. I opened my eyes as we floated together, coming face to face with something inhuman. The nose was out of place, the mouth a rictus hole of rotting teeth, the eyes where the chin should be. I didn't have the dream much but when I did, without fail, I awoke with a shriek.

The face was upside down, waggling back and forth like a grotesque bobble-head as it chittered insistent nonsense I didn't understand before moaning three words.

"Come with me," it said.

"Don't say it," Rayven said.

I said it anyway.

"Saves matches."

We turned right at the Columbus Co-Op, the last of the mom-and-pop grocery stores in Harris, passing under the lone streetlight shining above the store. Leaving Seventh Street, we continued down the dark sidewalk on Bogart Street, brushing invisible spider webs from our faces as we passed under the branches of low-hanging Maple trees, we came to my house on the corner of Bogart and Ninth. The festival seemed a million miles away. Finding my key to the back door under the patio light, we went inside to the kitchen. I pulled the refrigerator door open, bathing the room in shadows. At once, I stuffed my salami roll past containers of leftover spaghetti and meat loaf. Rayven slid his cheese wheel on the shelf below, pushing aside a container of potato salad and two boxes of Chinese take-out. I slammed the door shut, our victory at the Lion's Club booth long forgotten as we left the house, retracing our steps back to the Columbus Co-Op.

Standing under the streetlight wondering what to do next, Rayven pointed down the street with a yell.

"Hey! We can catch the tractor at Immigrant Square and go back down to Water Street!"

We did have round-trip tickets. It made sense.

The low roar of a John Deere tractor as it accelerated growled faintly over the street from the direction of the Wine Garden.

Breaking into a run, we headed in the opposite direction toward the Immigrant Fountain, three blocks away. Side-by-side we flew down the sidewalk, heads thrown back and sucking air as our feet slapped cement in a familiar rhythm I'd heard Dad play on his drum set.

L-R-R-L-RRR-LLL-RR-L-R-L-RR-LL-RRR

One block to go, I looked back. The tractor's headlights were in view. Lowering chin to chest, I poured it on, seeing Rayven's heels coming off the sidewalk and going down again over and over a couple feet in front of me.

Just before the sidewalk ended, we cut left at Pike Street.

Victory!

Skidding past the Coal Fountain and the Immigrant Statue, we lurched to a stop in front of the Flags of Many Nations. The stately display reminded me of what Mrs. Stringfellow had said in my second-grade class. *We honor those who came before.* An impressive cluster of thirty flagpoles stood tall, flags fluttering in the faint night air. The flags represented the nations of the forefathers who had come together to find the town of Harris. Hands on my knees, I gasped and spit, gulping air into desperate lungs. Glancing to my left, I saw Rayven on his knees, greedily slurping from the Bull Head Drinking Fountain under heaving shoulders.

We'd beat the tractor to Immigrant Square with time enough to recover and then some.

The tractor came into view, shambling down Seventh Street and cutting its gears as it turned onto Pike Street, carefully parking alongside the sidewalk. The diesel engine growled one last time as the tractor shut down. "Ten minutes, folks!" the driver announced from his metal perch. "Ten minutes!"

Rayven and I sat side-by-side on the edge of the Coal Fountain, regarding the tractor and the disembarking passengers with amusement as they milled over Immigrant Square to study and marvel at its memorial structures. I wondered how many of the people were first-time riders, how many had come from out of town. I wondered what their lives were like, beyond the festival, beyond this moment in time, these people I would never see again but felt connected to in a way I couldn't understand. I felt myself smile.

This is something special, I told myself.

Remember this moment.

I turned to Rayven, planning to put my arm over his shoulder, to explain away the gesture as confirmation of our shared victory over the tractor ride, but he was gone.

Strangers had gathered around the Coal Fountain. Some threw coins into the pool below the waterfall, others took pictures of family and friends posing stiffly in front of the towering cylinder of coal. I was surrounded by crowds of people edging up to the fountain, Rayven nowhere in sight. I stood up and walked sideways between the crowd until I could see the sidewalk, the tractor beyond, its two wagons empty. I turned around and scanned the scene. There were too many people milling over Immigrant Square to make out any single person. What the hell had happened to Rayven? Where was he?

I thought about calling his name, but before I could, I felt a hand touch my back just above my jeans and I whirled around, startled.

"Hey, Julian."

"Hi!" I said automatically as I turned, before seeing who stood before me.

The first thing I noticed was her slight, slender body, almost a foot shorter than me. She wore homemade cut-off jeans, a trick families used to prolong the life of clothes, and a black Led Zeppelin t-shirt, accented with strands of dark auburn hair.

It was Casey Woodruff.

I tried to sound casual. "How's it going?"

Then I saw something I'd never seen Creepy Casey do before.

I saw her smile.

"It's going," she said, tilting her head and nodding. "Yeah, it's going all right. How about you?"

I shrugged, then pointed to the tractor, then my arms were all over the place, unsure of what they should do. I put my hands in my pockets. Took them out again. Scratched my nose. Pinched the front of my sweaty shirt off my chest and waggled it to generate cool air. Raised one arm to gesture at the Coal Fountain while still shaking my shirt with other. Spread my damp hair back behind my head with both hands.

"We raced the tractor here," was all I could say, remembering my dreams-turned-nightmares of this weird girl, dreams warning me she was someone to be avoided, somehow an imminent danger to...to...*something*.

Arms at her side, she slid her feet two steps toward me, the tips of her black flats connecting with the front of my Vans.

She looked up into my face with wide, searching eyes.

"Did you win?"

I leaned forward. Maybe I started to swoon. I don't know. There wasn't time to think before I was pulled back by a muscular arm around my neck. And there was Rayven, his face afire with his usual exploding toothy grin.

"BET YOUR BUTT WE WON! BY FIVE MINUTES AT LEAST!"

What had happened? I had to blink, once, then a second time harder and longer to get my bearings. Rayven held me to his side, repeatedly shaking me as he laughed and laughed. Cami and Evie stood in front of him, all smiles.

"We heard your dad playing inside the Wine Garden," a male voice said. My head spun around as if on a lazy Susan, coming to rest on the figure of a man dressed in an Izod shirt and Bermuda shorts.

"This is Mr. Woodruff," Rayven introduced. I took the man's hand, feeling myself shake it out of numb reflex.

"I'm Michael," Mr. Woodruff said. "Good to meet you at last. Your dad's one hell of a drummer!"

I mumbled a *thank you*.

A woman appeared from behind Mr. Woodruff. Although not identical, she was dressed like Mr. Woodruff: a denim skirt and loose white blouse. Comfortable attire for enjoying the festival. Suburban. Financially comfortable, yet nowhere near wealthy. Just regular people living their lives who had gained some weight around the hips and stomach without a hint of pretension.

Regular people.

"I'm Casey's mom, Jean." She shook my hand. "We're hoping to catch your dad's band next month in Rosedale. We promised the kids a slumber party this weekend, so no Wine Garden for us!" She gave me a look of mock disappointment, then let out a little laugh.

I returned a wan half-smile, still feeling disoriented, dizzy.

"Nice to finally meet you, Julian." She put her free hand over mine, giving our clasped hands a squeeze.

The pleasantries complete, Mrs. Woodruff abruptly turned. She motioned down the street toward the neighborhood beyond Immigrant Square. "Let's go girls!"

Cami and Evie waved their goodbyes to us as they headed down Thirteenth Street to the Woodruff home.

I frowned. Someone was missing.

Mr. Woodruff stood in front of me, blocking my view of the others.

"Have fun, Julian, be careful. We'll see you boys later," he said, stepping away to follow his wife. As he turned, there was Casey.

She'd been standing behind him since Rayven and the rest of them had greeted me. *Did you win?* she'd asked. After that, she seemed to vanish. Now here she was again.

She raised her palm between her serious face and mine, waving a stiff goodbye, her hand rocking slowly back and forth before falling in line behind her father. One of the twins called back in a faraway voice, "Casey, come on!" and this strange girl bolted down the street to join her slumber party friends, looking back ever so slightly with a glance I knew was meant for me.

───────────

Instead of going all the way back to Water Street's booth and bustle, we hopped off the tractor ride at the Wine Garden. There was no music coming from within and dozens of people milled around on the sidewalk in front of the entrance, smoking and drinking. Scattered cliques standing in ragged circles chatting it up, releasing intermittent whoops and hollers.

I looked across the street beyond the first wagon hitched to the parked tractor next to where I stood, seeing the neon clock shining electric red between the tops of the mechanic bay doors at Arcomo's Sinclair. Ten thirty-six.

The Strays were between sets, taking a break with two more sets to go. For the folks at the Wine Garden, the party was in full swing, but the night had just begun.

I scanned the people surrounding us hoping to see Dad even as I knew he was still within the bowels of the Garden, hanging out with Finny and the rest of the band. Rayven was on the edge of the crowd at the far side of the building, motioning me to him.

"I got an idea," he said. Reaching into his pocket, he pulled out a wadded bill, pulling it open with a *snap!* between his hands. "Lookee what I got."

He held the wrinkled ten-dollar bill proudly in front of him. "I say we head over to Dreamland. It'll be so busy; I can score us a six-pack no problem."

I knew he was right. The tavern would be filled to overflowing. Rayven was big for his age, tall and chiseled and confident. He'd have no trouble flashing the ten and coming out with the beer.

"We can go behind Pastore Lumber and have a grand old time."

Right again. It was a great idea. Close enough to the revelries of the festival yet hanging out in a place we'd never be caught, two underage guys drinking beers in the dark where we could still hear the tractor's roar, the shouts, the music, the Harley's growling over the streets while we partied, invisible to everyone. My body tingled. Courting danger with little consequence.

I forgot about Dad as we passed along the side of the Wine Garden. A block later, I mingled with the overflow of Dreamland patrons on the sidewalk, shuffling around to one side with my head down, trying to avoid attention. Trying to look...*invisible.* I thought suddenly of Casey Woodruff. Of her effortless invisibility back at Immigrant Square. Mostly, I thought of that final glance over her shoulder at me. Her face more sad than sinister, a mixture of...*other things.*

Rayven came out of Dreamland clutching a swollen brown paper bag under one arm and I fell in step with him as we headed to Pastore Lumber. "*Two* six-packs," he whispered out of the corner of his mouth. "And I got change back."

"Shitfire," I hissed through gritted teeth. Muffled clanking of bottles rang out from the bag under Rayven's arm as we broke into a slow jog.

"Damn right," he said.

An hour later with eight bottles of Falstaff beer left, we were well entrenched behind Pastore Lumber, lounging on the ground against a stack of pallets and on our way to getting proper drunk.

Opening another Falstaff against a pallet board, my palm over the neck as I snapped off the cap, I caught the overflow of foam in my mouth, swallowing greedily. Rising, I headed beyond the mast lights of the lumberyard into the darkness of the dirt road leading up Crumpton Hill. Behind me, I could see Rayven stretched out on the ground, gulping Falstaff from his bottle with abandon.

"Let's go up to your house," I called to the tiny image of Rayven sitting against the pallets, legs splayed over the ground. I was invisible again, twice in one night. *Beat that,* came a thought out-of-nowhere about Casey Woodruff.

"Dude, it's a ten-minute drive to my house," Rayven yelled back. "That's an hour's walk at least. Besides, the place is locked up tight. No one's home." He drained the bottle and threw it aside. "Nothin' up there except a buncha woods." He opened another Falstaff. "C'mon back here. You've been there anyway." He took a pull on the bottle, swallowed, and coughed. "What're you talking about?"

Rayven retrieved three empty bottles, putting his index finger down the neck of one, then his middle and ring fingers into the other two. He started clanking them together, the brittle sound ringing over the deserted lumberyard.

"Warri-ors..come out to playee-yah," his shrill voice sang.

Emerging from the light, I became visible again.

"There you are," he declared in his normal voice.

"Great movie."

"Yes, sir," he said, raising the finger bottles to toast our shared taste in the movie. Giving them two *clanks*, he whipped his arm to one side, launching the bottles from his fingers into a thick patch of weeds beyond. Rayven waited until I'd taken up my seat next to him again before answering his own question. *"I know what you're talking about."*

I opened another beer. The bottle had lost its chill and I knew what was coming before I took the first swig. The flavor was as satisfying as warm piss. The liquid expanded like a balloon in my mouth and the bottle bubbled over, tepid foam running over my hand. I swallowed hard, tasting the foul lukewarm brew in my nostrils.

29

"You've been up to my house," Rayven continued. "You've been up there a hundred times. We've explored the woods, grilled hamburgers, played badminton, and thrown the football. We've watched movies together, you name it. You name it because you know it. We've done it for years, dude."

I took another pull from the bottle, a smaller one this time as I tried to formulate my response. A response to what started to seem like a forced argument, as a solution looking for a problem. Yet I had a nagging feeling there was a mystery inside our lives, maybe one much larger than our circumstances, larger than ourselves, the people we knew, our families, friendship, and even love. Maybe the mystery was hidden deep within some forgotten legacy of Harris, Indiana itself.

"And we've had plenty of sleepovers," he finished.

I sat upright. There it was. The crack my response had been searching for.

"Yeah, but not—*never*—at your house."

Rayven burst into hearty laughter, staring directly at me. The laughter stopped almost as soon as it began. His face was still and pensive, eyes narrowed in bewilderment.

"*Dude.* That's between you and your dad."

Rayven slid next to me, close enough that we seemed connected as Siamese Twins, our shoulders and outstretched legs touching. I suddenly understood he was reacting to my lack of response, or rather to my silent response which had overwhelmed not only my face, but my entire body. I felt as if I had seen a ghost, died of fright or both.

"Uncle John's never told you," Rayven said aloud, but his words came out flat, audible thoughts not meant to be heard.

I shook my head and took another drink. This time, the beer was Ambrosia and soothing. I took another mouthful, swallowed, and felt my breath steady into an easy rhythm.

"Look, Julian, our dads, I don't know what it is. They're brothers, you know? They *share* things we can only guess at. Like we do, like these beers here, you know? With my folks, they made their own decisions, different ones for me and my sisters and Uncle John and you. I just figured your dad must have told you, you know?"

30

I stared down the narrow neck of the Falstaff bottle clutched tightly in both hands. "I don't know anything."

"Okay, like Evie and Cami's friend, the girl we saw—"

"*Casey.*" Her name felt like unrefined cane sugar spilling over my lips.

"Yeah, her. She's spent the night at our house before, lots of times. They always camp out in the pavilion in the yard. I don't hang out with them. I'm in the house with Mom and Dad. I guess they have a good time, how the hell do I know? The next morning, they go down the hill to take her home and that's that."

"No," I argued. "That's not that. The only friends Casey has are your sisters. Everywhere else, she's shunned like she's some kind of monster. There's Cam and Eve, you and I and my dad and Uncle Vincent and Aunt Laurie and even Casey's parents. We're all regular people compared to her."

Rayven grabbed the last two unopened bottles of Falstaff and stood up. "We can drink these on the way back to your house," he said. "Toss 'em in some backyard before we get there."

I finished my bottle, threw it aside and wrapped my hand around Rayven's hand and the fresh bottle in his grip. "You're not telling me everything."

He shook his head. "You're right. You'll have to ask your dad because he knows."

Relaxing my hand, I took the offered bottle.

"I will tell you this, dude, for what it's worth."

His face glowed a shimmering pale under the mast lights of the lumberyard.

"The Bakers—I mean our families. We're *of* the hill. Period. Everyone else, well, they just go *up* the hill."

Rayven took me by the shoulders.

"You handle it how you can. You handle it in your way."

He pulled me close, whispering in my ear.

"Things come out at night up there, cousin. Ask your dad."

Chapter Four

Father and Son

I'm not sure that Dad ever wanted to be a father. Or even a husband, for that matter. But long before I came into the picture, John Baker, the person, had committed to both roles, vowing to do his best. This was no small task.

Like his older brother, Vincent, John stubbornly clung to his ways. Both siblings were misfits from an early age as far as the accepted norms of conformity. From Kindergarten on, Vincent was formal and reserved while Dad was the free-spirited hell-raiser. Always, they leaned and relied on each other with Vincent providing his extra thirty-six-month knowledge to John. It was as if they were twins. Or maybe best friends who had been reincarnated over and over again always finding themselves in the same roles. Vincent was the first to marry and the first to have children while Dad pursued his dream of being a professional musician, adding my mom to the mix. To all accounts theirs was a whirlwind love affair which only stopped when Mom died, leaving John alone with a toddler and his broken heart. He rose to that commitment as well, I suspect from a combination of his love for Mom and the support of his brother, my Uncle Vincent. While my mother's absence was a daily presence in my life, Dad covered all the bases. My childhood was filled with a sense of love and security. Aunt Laurie was always around to tamp down my vague desire for a mother. Uncle Vincent, on the other hand, remained a mystery. My first memory of him was that of a spectral figure, a ghostly mist of sorts, always in the background of my landscape. They visited us frequently. Aunt Laurie always came with cookies or brownies or fudge, always with a beaming smile and the most wonderful hugs. Meanwhile, Uncle Vincent was always in the background, catching me in his sideways glance and narrowed eyes as he went off with Dad to another room.

Rayven and I were eight years old before we realized we were related. A year later, I realized he had two younger sisters, Evie and Cami and that we all were related. John and Vincent Baker were our fathers. When you're young, life is funny like that, rapidly unfolding surprising mysteries on an almost daily basis. For most people, the mysteries are solved and dry up early on, leaving only the rest of life. Not so for the Baker brothers and their children.

My dad had both every expectation and no expectation for me and he told me so from an early age. "There's nothing you can't do," I remember him telling me. "Whatever you want to be, you can be. It's out there for the taking. The hardest job you'll ever have is figuring that out because you have to figure it out early on."

Dad was not religious or political in the extreme as far as I knew. Whatever biases he held he kept to himself, offering a poem by Philip Larkin instead, one which he often repeated in a quiet earnest voice:

They fuck you up, your mum and dad.
They may not mean to, but they do.
They fill you with the faults they had
And add some extra, just for you.
But they were fucked-up in their turn.
By fools in old-style hats and coats
Who half the time were soppy-stern.
And half at one another's throats.
Man hands on misery to man.
It deepens like a coastal shelf.
Get out as early as you can,
And don't have kids yourself.

He would burst into laughter at the end while I clapped madly. We repeated this ritual through the years, never tiring of the timeless profundity of Larkin's poem. Our private ceremony always ended in a mutual hug, a tight embrace I hoped would never end. Always in my ear was Dad's voice. "I love you, son. More than anything. I love you."

———————

"Hey! You guys up?"

On the floor next to my bed, I heard Rayven snoring in the sleeping bag.

I pulled the covers tighter over me against Dad's voice. Could it be morning already? From under the covers, I knew by the close sound of Dad's voice he was standing in the doorway of my room, regarding me and his nephew, two lumps under disheveled blankets who had spent one great, one hell-of-a-night, roaming the Little Italy Festival.

"I see a nice new salami and cheese wheel in the refrigerator. I'm about to grab a knife and eat it all if no one claims it."

I pulled the covers off my face, head still pressed into my pillow. "Should've seen it, Dad," I said in a sleepy voice with closed eyes. "What a win. Rayven and me at the same time."

I felt the mattress compress as Dad sat down at the foot of the bed, felt his hand on my shoulder. His voice was soothing and gentle. "Your Uncle Vincent told me. Wish I could have been there."

"It was something to see," I mumbled. Dad's hand ran over the top of my head.

"Sounds like it for sure," he agreed. "Listen, I gotta run to the Wine Garden for a while, make sure the gear is set for tonight and then me and Finny are gonna grab some lunch at Terra Villa. I'll be back around two to run Rayven home, okay?"

"Sure, Dad."

"Make sure you guys are up and ready."

"Sure, Dad," I repeated. He threw the cover back over my head and gave me a slap on the back.

"See you in a few."

I felt the mattress expand as he stood up. Before falling back to sleep, I called to him from under the blanket.

"You sounded great last night. Great as always, Dad."

Whether he heard me or not, I didn't know.

The fastest way to Uncle Vincent's house from Harris was up Crumpton Hill, a narrow dirt road behind the Pastore Lumber Yard. Steep and treacherous in the best of conditions, Crumpton Hill was avoided by most everyone since the only thing at the very top was thick woods and the house itself. The only other route to the house was from Rosedale on the other side of the hill. But it was twenty miles from Harris to Rosedale on the main roads, then another four miles of gravel to the center of Crumpton Hill, where the house stood. Technically, the house was considered part of Rosedale rather than Harris, although Harris was much closer and seemed the logical address. The only people who ever used the gravel road from Harris up Crumpton Hill were Uncle Vincent and my dad.

More single-lane path than road, the way was washboard-rough and dusty on clear days or else a treacherous, greasy mess during and shortly after storms of either rain or snow. Forever going up, up, up, at a certain point you didn't want to look back toward Harris, no matter the weather. At certain points, one felt as if their vehicle would suddenly lose ground and careen backwards out-of-control to come crashing down to certain doom, colliding with one of the Pastore Lumber buildings and exploding into flames. The drive was like a rollercoaster from Hell. At least that's what it felt like to me, having never driven the road myself, always a passenger. Dad never seemed to mind, humming to himself and smoking a couple of cigarettes along the way, absently jerking the steering wheel right and left to avoid the larger potholes. I'd made the trip countless times, yet there was always a sense of imminent danger, my body tense with a constant throbbing of unease. By the time we reached Uncle Vincent's house, my feet would be numb after being locked hard against the floorboard for the fifteen-minute drive.

As Dad piloted our stripped-down Jeep Cherokee up the rough incline of Crumpton Hill, numb feet and sore ankles were the least of my worries. Looking over my shoulder at Rayven in the back seat clutching his cheese wheel, his sickly pale face echoed how I felt. We'd made it back home after polishing off—*how many?*—beers behind Pastore Lumber. I remember that much. I remember opening the front door. After that, I remember waking up. Now, here I was in the front seat next to Dad, trying my best to act nonchalant, forcing my body to slump casually against the backrest disguising a throbbing hangover I knew Rayven felt as sure as I did.

Halfway up the hill, I focused on Dad's profile. His body was a study in determination and focus as he steered the Jeep ever upward. One steely eye squinted against the road and the way ahead. One nostril flared every once in a while as he navigated a particularly rough spot, the Jeep bucking sharply up and down. His knuckles went from pink to white and back again as his hands finessed the steering wheel and gear shift. One foot pressed the clutch, then the brake pedal in unison with the other foot pressing the gas pedal. I watched him, mesmerized.

It was like he was dancing.

At once, the incline disappeared and we were at the top of Crumpton Hill, in Uncle Vincent's backyard. The summit of Crumpton Hill spanned twenty-five acres of mostly overgrown woods and Vincent owned it all. Only the backyard was cleared, a roughly manicured acre surrounded by tall maples and evergreens. Near the edge of the backyard was The Playhouse, a Quonset Hut-style shelter Dad and Vincent had built years before, intending it to be an outdoor gathering place for barbecues and outdoor parties. Instead, the mostly steel frame and glass structure had become second living quarters to Rayven, Evie, and Cami, at least during warmer months. There were a few electrical outlets inside and a solid cement floor, but the space was mostly primitive and sparse. The glass walls and heavy canvas flaps instead of a proper doorway made The Playhouse feel like you were camping out as opposed to being in a proper building. The outside was adorned with strings of those tube-lights normally used for holiday decorations. A stone footpath led to the backdoor of the house. I'd spent many days there with Rayven, plotting childhood adventures into the woods from our "headquarters" as we whiled away elementary school weekend days. Within the last year or so, I knew that The Playhouse had hosted sleepovers with friends of the twins, notably Casey Woodruff.

Dad gunned the Jeep down the wide dirt trail, the burst of speed throwing us back into our seats as we came over the hill, passing The Playhouse to the front yard.

"Okay," Dad said under his breath, pulling the Jeep onto the paved driveway in front of the house. The smell of hot rubber and exhaust fumes lingered in the air, burning my nostrils. "Here you are, Rayven," Dad said in a triumphant tone, as if he were Jason ushering one of his Argonauts home.

"Thanks, Uncle John," Rayven said gathering his cheese wheel under one arm and climbing out.

Dad raised his index finger at him in a casual salute. Then he said something I didn't understand, vaguely striking me as dishonest.

"Tell your mom and dad I'll see 'em later. Have to get back to the Wine Garden for tonight's show." Without waiting for an answer, he put the Jeep in reverse and backed down the driveway, but instead of heading around the house to descend Crumpton Hill, the Jeep reached the mailbox at the end of the driveway and Dad turned onto the smooth gravel road toward Rosedale.

The Jeep's clock read 3:10. Dad had picked us up at the house a little after two and now we were heading back through Rosedale, which would put us back in Harris well before four 'o clock. The Strays wouldn't take the Wine Garden stage for another five hours. By his own admission, Dad had already checked his gear and had lunch with Finny, so why had he told Rayven he had to get back? I sat in silence for the four miles until we hit the paved county highway, until my growing anxiety festered into a mute panic bordering on hysteria upon understanding I had just witnessed my father lie for the first time in my life. I looked sideways at Dad, my eyes wide. He was like a mannequin in the driver's seat, unmoving, stiffly facing forward, both hands locked over the steering wheel at twelve and two. It was like a dream. Or a nightmare. I blinked and suddenly Dad's hair was blowing behind him, carried by a soft warm wind. The Jeep picked up speed. He shifted in the seat and turned his head to me, revealing a bloodless face, dead and staring.

"*Glaboo-bottla-batta.*"

My jaw dropped at the gibbering sound. A scream stuck in my throat, held back by a glob of phlegm rattling deep in my throat. Instinctively, my hands went to my chest, fingers clutching the seatbelt for dear life. Dad's right hand came off the steering wheel reaching for me and pointed behind my seat.

"In my bag. Should still be cold."

My right arm reached back between my seat and the door. Immediately, I felt the open duffel bag, my fingers crawling over the plastic of a bottle of water. Gripping it hard, I pulled it from the bag and brought it forward.

A bottle of water.

Dad was facing forward once again, eyes on the road and slumped back into his seat as the Jeep moved arrow-straight down the county highway.

Nothing but a bottle of water.

Dad shot me a glance and smiled. "Got it. Good."

The chill of the bottle filled my palm, moving up my arm. It seemed just what I needed to soothe my throbbing head and body, aching from the Falstaffs of the night before. Fun while it lasted, but now a *bottla-botta* was just the thing. I cracked the cap and poured the ice-cold water down my throat.

I heard Dad say "You guys had a time last night, huh? Twelve pack or a case?"

I took a breath as the water ran cold down my throat and started to answer. How did he know? Had we been *that* obvious?

That *sloppy?*

"Doesn't matter," Dad said, as if he were talking to himself. Or someone else. He knew Rayven and I had capped off our great festival night with all its triumphs and mysteries, by getting drunk. "You did it up and that's that. All that matters, all that's real, is that you're okay right now."

Then it came to me. Rayven and I hadn't been that obvious or sloppy. We did it up, as Dad said, but his words were meant for a time long before Rayven scammed the Dreamland bartender and we sat behind Pastore Lumber pounding our bottles of Falstaff.

Dad was talking to himself. About himself.

Then, without warning, Dad started talking about me.

"Rayven's your buddy." It was a statement in no uncertain terms. Dad glanced at me, took his right hand off the steering to give my leg a pat. "I always hoped for that. Your Uncle Vincent, too. You guys were born just weeks apart—" Dad raised his head, sending a happy half-laugh skyward—"we were beside ourselves, your uncle and me. Both fathers to a son. No matter what else was going on, we had *that*. I remember leaning into your mother's face in the maternity room, I took her face in my hands and I was crying and I said, 'He's perfect.' We all knew there was something to it, me and your mom, Uncle Vincent and Aunt Laurie. *Two sons* born so close together. We agreed then, the four of us, we made a pact, that we wouldn't interfere as parents. Friend or foe, sink or swim, you boys would grow up and either come together or not on your own without any interference from us."

"Rayven's my best friend," I managed just above a whisper. "But he knows something, Dad—"

"Something you don't," Dad interjected.

I straightened in the seat. "Yeah, he knows something."

"Not as much as he thinks," Dad said. "But more than you."

"Yeah."

Dad nodded. "Only about Crumpton Hill, son. Only about the top of that...that wicked pile of dirt where they live."

The Jeep was suddenly in Harris; in fact, it was passing by the Wine Garden, close to our house. I hadn't so much as noticed the time or miles passing and here we were.

Dad pulled an open pack of cigarettes from his shirt pocket, took one into his mouth before replacing the pack. Unlit, it hung in the corner of his mouth. His teeth pinched the filter. "Julian, my son. My only beloved son. I'm gonna tell you what Rayven thinks he knows and then some." He grabbed a lighter from the console, lit the cigarette and puffed a thick cloud of smoke in front of his face, throwing the lighter back into the console as the Jeep turned onto our street.

"I'm gonna tell you everything."

Chapter Five

The Black Diamond Coal Mine

In 1941, Harris, Indiana was the definition of a *Boom Town*. The average family was flush with cash. The scourge of the economic downfall which had spread its curse over the nation, later to be termed *The Great Depression*, was fast losing the brutal grasp it had held over desperate citizens throughout the country for over a decade. For most of that time, the people of Harris weathered the indignity of the mass financial downturn because of the coal mines. Because, as folks said seated around kitchen tables and relaxing on living room davenports in homes throughout Harris, as far back as 1934, there was always work in the mines.

Indeed, there was.

And the work paid well. A coal miner with a wife and two children could rest assured that his family had every amenity they could want. Every amenity their neighbor enjoyed, who was likely a fellow coal miner. Unlike the mountain enclaves in West Virginia, or the primitive frontier towns in Colorado such as Ludlow, places springing from the whole cloth promise of the mining industry, Harris was an established town of merchants long before the mining industry arrived. There was Giacoletto's Gas Station and Bicycle Repair Shop. Bonacorsi's Market and the Columbus Co-Op grocery store and butcher shop. The Terra Villa Restaurant. The Palace movie theater. Dreamland Tavern. The town was well-established by the time the Great Depression was ravaging the rest of the country, so when the Black Diamond Coal Mine was opened, it came without the company stores and slave-labor working conditions so common in those other areas. Working in the mines, a job available to any able-bodied man, was just another opportunity to better one's family. Even Mutt, the butcher at the Columbus Co-Op, who had come from northern Italy as a child to Ellis Island and then to Harris, split his time between cutting meat in a brightly lit and surgically clean butcher shop to swinging a pickaxe in the filthy black dust of a narrow hole hundreds of feet underground, where the darkness knows no end. Mutt went from cutting meat every day to every third day and his customers adjusted to the change with ease. Working in the mines paid well, so Mutt's change in schedule as the only butcher in town was understood by everyone. After all, everyone knew someone who took up a job as a miner and they were as likely to be a family member as they were a neighborhood butcher.

The Black Diamond Coal Mine was the icing on the cake for a community who had struggled through and survived the devastating hardships still faced by most of the country. Everyone celebrated the good fortune the mine represented. Everyone took the reins with both hands, riding what they saw as a change for the better, hanging on to that better change for dear life as it galloped forward to an eventual worse no one saw coming until it was too late to dismount, too late to forestall a tragic destiny that would last for untold generations.

Thursday, June 27th, 9:48am, 1942.
Two minutes after the explosion

There was an ear-splitting rumble lasting a single second, followed by an eternity of screams from thirty-six grown men.

Checko Muciarelli pressed his knees to his chest harder than he ever thought possible, feeling his spine, curled over his body, shiver uncontrollably. The fingers of both hands clasped together over the back of his head as his open mouth struggled to find a single breath of air at the floor, breathing in and out to find only dust and grit building in his throat. He choked, spit, then coughed and then a deeper cough, a rasping, guttural reflex making him raise his head. He hocked a thick glob of bitter phlegm into his mouth and spat the foul wad on the invisible ground, putting one hand into the moist sludge and clawing backward, pushing himself forward. He was near the elevator, he knew that much, disoriented as he was. He was near the elevator. But not as close as the shrieks he clawed himself toward in the darkness. Someone was closer when the explosion happened. Whoever was screaming was closer to the elevator and the screams told Checko that the elevator was no longer the way out of the mine.

"*Hallo!*" Checko coughed out toward the elevator. But it was as if the word stopped in front of his nose, unable to move forward. He imagined it hanging there, the unseen letters floating in front of his blind eyes caught in a black web of coal-dust fog only to be swallowed up. The darkness was of such complete pitch that even his body felt unreal. He moved his hands in front of his face without so much as a shadow or shift of air, causing him to question where exactly his hands were or if they were even moving. Then, he lost all sense of up or down, right or left. The absence of pain, rather than comforting him, caused Checko momentary panic, adding to the sensation of numbness, of being disembodied yet conscious wrapped in a darkness without end. Reflexively, he gathered his arms to his chest and bowed his head to curl up, wishing himself small enough to disappear. His helmet connected with the ground, flickering the miner's light back to life.

Misty shades of dull black and brown objects large and small and every shape in between splashed over his eyes as if a velvet curtain had suddenly parted, filling his blurry vision. Impossibly close, like gazing through a microscope. He blinked once.

Rocks. Smaller pebbles. Dirt.

He could feel his knees pressed together underneath him, stinging from the gravel grating against his pants. He felt his elbows bent, tense arms crossed over his chest, his hands clenched under his chin. He felt himself able to see.

Curled up in the dirt, the angry dust falling and settling around him, a blessed urgency of feeling once more returned to him and Checko Muciarelli, still frozen in place, began to cry.

———————

Thursday, June 27th, 10:30am, 1942
Forty-six minutes after the explosion

From what Checko could see with the faint light from his helmet, the main cable of the elevator was intact, still holding arrow-straight leading up to the ground-level shaft. *That has to be a good thing*, he reasoned. *Has to be.* He squinted at the cable for a time, willing himself a measure of hope with his steely glare on the greased black thick rope of steel that could get them out of here. As bad as it was, that straight cable was better than the shitshow where he stood.

The elevator itself was a mess. One mangled side of the cage was pitched cockeyed into the mine, protruding from the shaft. The chances of it being used to evacuate everyone was next to nothing. But the cable itself could maybe be used to rig some kind of smaller hoist from above, maybe get the men out one at a time, but get them out just the same. In the meantime, the only thing Checko could do was help Mutt. The butcher's right arm was pinned against the wall of the mine and the ruined side of the elevator, effectively trapping him against rock and iron.

Mutt had screamed himself hoarse by the time Checko reached him, passing out from the pain only to wake again and emit slow-rolling steady moans.

"I got you," Checko said when he reached Mutt. He cradled his head in his hands, wiped strands of wet hair back from Mutt's forehead. "I got you Mutt. It's me, Checko."

Mutt tried to laugh, but it came out as a pain-filled groan of relief. His left arm reached out and grabbed the tail of Checko's shirt. "Checko. That's funny. What happened?"

"I think there was an explosion. Yeah, there was an explosion."

44

"That's funny," Mutt said again. "Here we are, checker and butcher. Co-workers."

"Friends," Checko said. "You're gonna be okay, Mutt. I'm here now."

"I know. Friends. What're the odds of that, you and me? What happened?"

"There was an explosion."

"A big one. It was something else. Boy, it sure hurts. I'm glad you're here, Checko."

"I know," Checko said. "I'm glad I'm here, too."

Thursday, June 27th, 1:05pm, 1942
Two hours, fifty-six minutes after the explosion

Mutt Generro would never cut meat with the surgical precision he once had, Checko knew that much was certain. He looked over the top of Mutt's head resting against his chest, to what he could see of the man's trapped arm. Through the ever-present mist of coaldust still floating around them, he could just make out Mutt's arm behind the elevator. Although still intact, the arm looked broken in at least two places and the fingers were mashed together, compressed under the iron screen in a grotesque approximation of a fist. Checko had tried everything he could think of to free Mutt's arm without success when the elevator lurched without warning.

Mutt came awake with a shriek. Checko grabbed him around the neck with one hand, his other hand on Mutt's pants, yanking him away from the elevator. Falling backward, he felt Mutt come away with him and gave out a triumphant yell as he hit the floor. Now he could put a tourniquet on Mutt's arm, he could lay his friend flat, he could give him some real help while they waited to be rescued. He heard himself say, "Gotcha, buddy. I gotcha."

Opening his eyes, Checko was alone on the ground.

Mutt, knees bent, swayed back and forth, his body banging first against the elevator, then the wall. His crushed arm was free to the elbow, but now there was a great wet bulge protruding from his right shoulder where the arm had dislocated from its socket. All Checko could do was stare.

Almost. Almost a good thing. I almost did a good thing. I almost did it. But I didn't and I'm sorry, as sorry as…as…sorry can be. I did my best and it wasn't enough and I'm as sorry as I'll ever be forever.

Checko got to his feet and went to Mutt, cupping one hand under Mutt's open mouth to catch the red drool spilling over a slack bottom lip of a lifeless body. The elevator bucked again and once more, Checko looking up at the main cable, still arrow-straight, as more and more dust began to rain down over him. The elevator suddenly broke loose and disappeared upward with an unearthly roar.

The last thing Checko saw was Mutt's body finally jerk free of the elevator, flailing toward him like a rag doll before spreading out in a wash of expanding gore as the mine entrance collapsed over them both.

Thursday, June 27th, 6:17pm, 1942
Eight hours, eight minutes after the explosion

Thirty-six men went into the Black Diamond Coal Mine that day, same as they had every day from 1936 to 1942 until the mine was closed forever after the explosion. Thirty-six men went in on that last day. One man came out. But that was never the story told to the children of Harris. The Black Diamond Coal Mine instead became legend and legacy, a story of heroes and sacrifice in service of our town. Checko Muciarelli was seventeen years old when he survived that horror. He went back to Columbus Co-Op, embracing his life as a checker for the next 70 years. He kept to himself, never married, lived modestly, and seemed to dedicate his life to the kids who came into the store by always sneaking them pieces of candy with a faraway smile before fanning his hand at them to go away. The first time I encountered

Checko, he was a slight, gray little man living on borrowed time who shuffled though the Co-Op aisles as if perpetually confused. Adults whispered his story about the coal mine, but Checko himself never spoke of his experience in the Black Diamond Coal Mine at all.

Except to one kid in particular.

Checko knew I'd lost my mother. Maybe Dad had told him, maybe it was common gossip at the time, I do not know. Maybe Checko absorbed quiet talk and hidden whispers like a sponge, sifting out what was important and what was not. The wheat from the chaff, so to speak.

Regardless, Checko took me under his wing and told me the story of what happened in the Black Diamond Coal Mine bit-by-bit. He was in his late eighties then, but the story he told was of a boy around my age. The story was tempered by time yet spanned the years between us. He was seventeen again and I was the wiser for the telling, way beyond my years.

Mutt Generro had been the first butcher at Columbus Co-Op. Dad didn't remember him except for the stories told to him by his father.

Everyone knew Checko Muciarelli, the sole survivor of the Black Diamond Mine tragedy. He passed away quietly in his little house on Second Street, two weeks to the day before Rayven and I had our adventures on the opening night of the festival. Beyond his obituary, there was an article in the Harris Observer about the mine tragedy and the history he represented. He was a beloved fixture of the town.

But no one knew him like I did. No one knew his story about what happened that day in 1942 like I did. Shortly after that balmy summer day in 1942, Harris, Indiana tried to erase the memory of the Black Diamond Coal Mine by naming the site that remained, Crumpton Hill.

Chapter Six

Secrets and Lies

U ncle Vincent was an insurance adjuster, whatever that was, and Aunt Laurie was a Human Resources Specialist for the State of Indiana, which I think meant she hired people.

Dad was the black sheep of the family.

"'Look at your brother,' your grandfather would say. 'Good grades, prospects. Why can't you be even half the kid Vincent is? I can't believe you're my son.' Now, your grandmother was not that direct. She was passive-aggressive to me. Hell, she was passive-aggressive to everyone in her life. They were both tortured in their own way, tortured through-and-through to their core. When you were born, they were different people. At least where you were concerned. It was often hard for me to believe they were the same people who raised me."

Frank and Martha Baker, my grandparents, both died a year after I was born. Three years later, my mother was gone as well.

"Your mom did her best to smooth out all the rough edges between me and my folks, rough edges that caused us to have some pretty knock-down drag-out battles ourselves. Your mom could never understand why I let my parents make me feel like I was still in competition with your uncle, like I was still a child. The funniest thing of all is that me and Vincent never felt that competition. We were joined at the hip from the start. Friends and comrades. Childhood co-conspirators. It was like my parents wanted us to hate each other, to be rivals forever. I could never understand that and looked to your mother to figure it out for me. That was a terrible burden I put on your mom. One of many. Your Mom. She sure was something else to put up with something like me. There I was, playing in bands like I was still in high school, even though I was responsible for a wife and child. I was drinking back then, doing a lot of drugs, living the whole rock n' roll bullshit while your mom worked a steady job, keeping us in everything we needed and more. What money I ever made, I spent on myself."

My Grandma, Martha, died within a few months of losing her husband. Their considerable assets were willed to the oldest son, Vincent. There was no provision for their younger son, John. There was no mention of him at all in that document.

"Your Uncle Vincent was beside himself. He was angrier than your mother, I think, and both were properly pissed at that will. I was just numb. I cared but I didn't, you know? Your mother expressed the anger she knew I couldn't express. Anyway, when Vincent sold their house in Allendale—the big one we drive past every now and then, the one I point out to you—he split the assets with me. That's when your mom and I bought this house with cash. Within two weeks, your Uncle Vincent bought the house on Crumpton Hill. And we both ended up with cash to spare, savings accounts that make the tellers at the First National Bank treat us like royalty to this day. I go in there carrying a coffee can half-full of dimes and quarters to pour into the change machine so I can deposit thirty bucks in my account and it's all 'hello, Johns' and 'yes, sirs', and 'how you doin', Mr. Baker's?'."

"So... we're *rich*?"

Dad fanned one arm over the kitchen in a flourish. "You tell me, son."

Sitting across from him at the worn kitchen table, its top stained and chipped by the ghosts of spilled milk and grape jelly and dropped forks, I followed his arm over the room. The refrigerator was older than me. The stove, the sink, and its faucet were the same as I'd always remembered, all older than me. The cabinets seemed dated, the dull linoleum floor gritty underfoot.

Before I could answer, Dad said, "We're okay."

49

I nodded.

"We're gonna stay that way," he added. He spread both arms out across the table. "Look at you, Julian." I thought I saw tears well in his eyes, but as fast as they came, they were gone. "I couldn't be prouder of you, son." He turned his head left and right to accent the point he was trying to make. Open palms pleaded to me over the table. "This isn't your future."

I was almost stopped by Dad's face, the sadness and contrition I'd seen there so many times before in different forms. Sometimes it came out as an apology for hurtful words spoken. Sometimes it begged my forgiveness for a missed function in school.

This time, I wasn't buying it.

I straightened against the back of the chair. Instead of taking Dad's hands, I folded my arms in my lap. "What is it, then, Dad?" I asked, staring at him defiantly. "What *IS* my future?"

Dad looked down at the table, not able to make eye contact with me.

"Mom's not here to help me with that question, Dad. She's not here to help you with your questions. She can't help anybody anymore. *Mom's gone*, Dad, she's dead and long gone."

After a beat, Dad drew a deep breath and looked at me.

"The whole town including me, told Vincent not to buy the house. It was an old house, built in the late fifties, beautiful in its time, but it was abandoned and rundown after being vacant for almost twenty-five years. Vincent and Laurie fell in love with the place, the possibilities of what they could make it. A three-story house, over four thousand feet of living space from top to bottom. Vincent spent every penny from his inheritance to make it what it is today."

"But what it used to be. It's still what it *used* to be, isn't it?"

Dad was silent.

"'*Things come out at night.*' that's what Rayven said. What, Dad? *What* comes out at night? You promised to tell me. 'I'm gonna tell you everything,' you said."

Dad pushed back against his chair. The chair legs protested with a sharp squeak away from the table as Dad stood up. He regarded me across the table, neither one of us speaking for a long time. I sat there staring up at him, vowing not to say a word. Dad continued to stare at me. I couldn't read his face or his eyes. He just looked at me. Standing there, he just stared at me. His body was flaccid but his eyes were searching as they moved over me. Finally, he opened his mouth and spoke.

"I'll answer every question you have I know the answer to, son. I'll tell you everything I know."

———————

Dad went to the refrigerator and took out two cans of beer, placing one in front of me. He took his seat again, the other beer in his hand. Motioning to me, he cracked the tab of his beer. I did the same.

"I abandoned you a lot through the years, Julian, to serve myself, to go after what I wanted," he said in a tone so formal it frightened me. "Other times, when I couldn't dismiss you, I rode your ass," he continued. "As much as I tried to honor your mother and be a good father, a good man, I know I've failed in so many stupid ways in which I know I could have done better. I can't fix the past, son, but I have to tell you I'm sorry."

"Dad…" I wanted to tell him that he was wrong, but he raised his hand to stop me.

"Against all odds, Vincent and Laurie made the house a true showplace. We all had money to spare after your grandparents died, so they spared no expense and in no time, the house was something to behold. It was spectacular. The house, the yard, all of it. At one point there was talk of designating the place as a National Historic Site."

He was barely able to get out the words *National Historic Site* before exploding into hoarse laughter hard enough to make his body shudder. He wiped a hand across his face, wagging his head in a futile attempt to clear the memory.

"That idea fell to shit pretty quick," he finished, trying to chuckle. It came out as a clutching sob from deep inside him, from a hidden cauldron of regrets it seemed he had been stirring for almost his whole life. "So much for the Baker Brothers making good."

But Uncle Vincent *had* made good, while Dad was busy being himself. Uncle Vincent was a success at his job, he and Aunt Laurie were deeply in love, they were raising three kids, never wanted for money…and now had a showplace atop Crumpton Hill, according to Dad's account so far.

I forgot about wanting to know whatever truth I was missing about Uncle Vincent's House, the "Big Secret" everyone except me seemed to already know and take in stride.

I started to think Dad was the problem. His ever-changing moods. His *Fly-By-The-Seat-of-Your-Pants* philosophy. Dad was like a planet everyone else just managed to orbit. Everyone else had to adjust their trajectory around Dad while he rotated on his own unchanging journey.

Scooting my chair backward, I stood up and went to the sink, emptying the almost full can of beer into the drain. Turning to Dad with the best dramatic flourish I could muster, I gave him a cold stare and declared I was going to bed.

I don't know what reaction I was expecting or hoped to get, only that my anger cloaked in some realization of Dad as some sort of all-encompassing villain would be justified by whatever happened. I was out of the kitchen, halfway through the living room, when I heard a voice I'd never heard before.

"Good-night, son. See you in the morning."

It was more than monotone. More than reserved. I think Dad himself would have admitted it was more than a self-pitying, somehow passive-aggressive sorry-not-sorry delivery. I turned around and gave him a cold stare. "Good-night, son, see ya in the morning," I mocked. Then I leaned forward with clenched fists and shouted, "You promised me everything and told me *nothing*, Dad! JUST LIKE ALWAYS!"

I waited there frozen yet shaking from head to toe with frustration. I still stared the man down, as if my stare held some kind of power over him. If I stared long enough, maybe Dad could give me answers to questions I didn't yet know.

"Fuck you," I heard myself say to him. I hadn't wanted to say it, wasn't sure if I even felt it, but the words came out all the same. No longer were my eyes on him. Instead, they studied the worn laminate floor in front of my feet.

"You promised me everything," I repeated in a softer voice. I was defeated. But not from what Dad had done or not done, what he had said or not said, but rather from myself. I was defeated at that moment by my own fear. By what I didn't yet understand and wasn't sure I wanted to ever know.

Dad said my name from a million miles away.

I looked up from the floor back to him. He was still sitting in his chair, same way as before I'd bolted from my own chair and left the room. He looked as defeated as I felt and sadder than sadness itself. His voice was barely above a whisper, hands folded on the table.

"This is new to me. It takes a while," he said, staring at me in earnest through watery eyes. "I have to be careful with this right now. Two people or ten or a hundred who experience the exact same thing will tell as many versions of what happened. They'll include their theories, their biases and what they think in the same experience, making it all lies. I don't want to do that. I don't want to lie anymore."

There was no anger from my *fuck you* comment or from my growing rage. Just an arm rising heavy off the table, a slow wave of a tired hand urging me to rejoin the conversation.

"The Truth takes some time, from me to you, anyway, where this whole thing…this…this whole…*mess* is concerned."

What choice did I have? I shuffled back to the kitchen table and took up my seat.

Dad wasted no time.

"We'd finished The Playhouse midday, our last project of so many. The place was done at last. It was perfect. So, me and your mom and Aunt Laurie and Uncle Vincent, each of us with infant sons, decided it was a good time to celebrate. So we had a cookout. We put you and Rayven in the same crib inside The Playhouse while we barbecued hamburgers and chicken legs on two Weber grills just outside the front of The Playhouse, so the four of us could watch you both and have a

53

grand old time all at once. We sat at the same picnic table that's still in the yard, the four of us."

"The picnic table off the stone path from The Playhouse to the back door of the main house," I said.

"That's right, only about thirty feet from where you guys were in that single crib. You both fell asleep before the sun went down. After that, me and your mom and your aunt and uncle were sitting around the picnic table, eating and drinking beer and having a helluva time."

Dad stopped and looked down at his hands. They were clasped together so tightly the knuckles were white.

"Your Mom saw them first. Standing at the edge of the woods staring at us. She was always composed, your mom. All she did was nudge my knee with hers to get my attention. She nodded her head toward the tree line."

He looked up at me. I'd never seen him scared before.

"At first, all I could see were the shadows of the tall trees in the dark. I said 'What?' a second before Vincent saw what your mom saw. He came off the picnic table so fast, he fell backward and hit the ground. Your Aunt Laurie screamed. I was the last to see them."

Dad inhaled deeply, his cheeks puffed out as he held his breath and then released a tremendous blow as he exhaled through pursed lips.

"It was Mom and Dad. Your grandparents. Both long dead and gone. Standing there clear as anything and staring at us with grim faces."

A guttural *humph* came from somewhere deep inside him as he shook his head at the memory.

"Your Mom and Aunt Laurie, well, they were freaked out of course. But for me and Vincent, it was more than that. I don't know if you can understand, but I can't explain it any better. *It was more.*"

Dad shrugged then.

"It was guilt, resentment, all our memories, our childhood slights, and the fucked-up way we were raised all coming back to me and Vincent at the same time. The shared memories and feelings we each felt, suddenly knowing those feelings had been justified all along. I remember getting up from the picnic table and going to Vincent, who was still flailing on the ground. I fell next to him, wrapping my arms around his shoulders and holding on for dear life. Your mom and Aunt Laurie ran into the house, wrapped in their own terror at the sight of two dead people, leaving us rolling around in the grass, reduced to two scared kids."

What the FUCK?!

I must have said it out loud because Dad raised his hand to stop me so he could continue.

"Your Uncle Vincent got us both to The Playhouse somehow, I don't know, my eyes were closed. I remember his hand pulling me to my feet, his fingers yanking my shirt collar and pinching the skin on my neck as he jerked us both into a stumbling run. I think we went airborne between the flaps of The Playhouse before crashing down inside. When I opened my eyes, I saw the phantasm of our parents standing at the picnic table, same as before at the edge of the woods. Only now, they were staring into The Playhouse, both of them pointing at us. And something else. *The sound came.* They spread blackened dead lips in unison, releasing low moans in our direction. Their wails filled the night and grew into an ear-splitting crescendo before turning away and moving toward the house like they were on roller skates. *They were floating.*"

I coughed out a breath of surprise, half out of my chair and realizing I was almost stretched over the kitchen table, awestruck. Dad reached out and took the side of my head in his palm.

I expected him to comfort me, to end his story by telling me it had just been a drunken dream they all thought they shared that night so many years ago.

Instead, he said, "There's more, son. Most of it you'll have to see for yourself. You'll have to try and figure it out best as you can. Finally, you'll have to make peace with it..."

"...as best as I can," I finished.

I fell back into my chair. Dad dropped his hand on the table, shaking his head.

"No," he breathed out. "*Any way* you can."

Things come out at night, I remembered Rayven saying.

55

All kinds of things.

Chapter Seven

Slumber Party

Pursued, the fox runs furiously toward the woods. In his haste, he makes a single mistake that proves to be fatal as the dogs, his pursuers, close in on him. That one mistake seals his doom.

The fox is elegant as he runs, darting through the trees and low brush. He's a faster animal than those on his tail, the barking canines, the whooping hunters. He knows the surrounding forest better than he knows himself, certainly more than those following behind him as he ducks one way and darts another. Still, he keeps running until he is sure he's covered enough ground to leave whatever is chasing him behind. The fox stops to take a breath before glancing back at the last thing his eyes will ever see before he is caught and killed.

The mistake which caused the death of the fox wasn't that he didn't run fast enough. Wasn't that he took the wrong path or stopped to catch his breath. Wasn't that he looked back.

No.

What sealed the doom of the fox was that he left his den in the first place. Had the fox stayed put while the horsemen and dogs passed by, the hunt would have ended with conciliatory handshakes from the riders and tired dogs slurping from pans of cool water, both having lost their quarry. But it was a frightening, thunderous sound inside the fox den as the dogs and hunters passed over the ground above and the fox was overcome with fear and therefore couldn't think straight and so he bolted.

A bullet from one of the riders pierced his shoulder, causing him to tumble and then the dogs were upon him, tearing him apart. As he struggled to his last flailing paw, the fox understood that fear had killed him. Fear had led him to make the decision which bore this final consequence—the dogs barking and snapping as they chewed him to pieces. Wide, liquid eyes glazed over, passing into death and that was all.

The fox was doomed once it left its den.

Once it decided to try and outrun its own fear.

A simple enough lesson.

———————

A month later, after the Little Italy Festival had faded into distant memory along with the salami I'd won, Dad and I were on the driveway changing the oil in the Jeep. Even our conversation about Uncle Vincent's house seemed insubstantial and unreal, like a dream.

"This damn Pitcock won't budge," Dad grumbled under the Jeep. I studied his feet poking out from the creeper, hoping they would telegraph what I should do.

"You need the ball peen?" The hammer was already in my hand as I knelt in front of the grille.

I heard Dad grunting as he tried again to loosen the drain plug and failed. "Yeah, I think that'll get it."

I reached under the grille, hammer in hand. "Here you go."

He began beating the shit out of the socket wrench handle. Several metallic clangs and a couple of *Goddammits* later, the drain plug came loose and I heard Dad say "Yeah, baby," in the *Not-Quite-Whisper Voice* I'd heard many times before.

When I was younger, Dad did the Voice a lot out of frustration when he couldn't get his point across. *Clean your room,* he would tell me. When he came back to find I hadn't cleaned my room, he would say "Goddamn it, Julian, I TOLD you to clean this goddamn room!" Then, he would walk away, getting just far enough down the hallway before saying under his breath in the *Not-Quite-Whisper Voice* , "Fucking kid ain't gonna amount to nothin'."

Disguised as a comment Dad was making to himself, he made sure it was loud enough for his target to hear. Dad finally talked about it with me a couple years back and we had a laugh. But it was something he used to do a lot to Mom, too, he confessed, even to Vincent occasionally. Although we both treated it as something funny from the past, I knew that deep down, Dad was ashamed and confused about why he had ever started doing the Voice in the first place. After Mom died, he never used the Voice again, but sometimes I recognized the same tone in less egregious, harmless situations.

The creeper slid from under the Jeep and Dad stood up, beaming. "Yeah, I know," he said, seeing my accusing smile.

I handed him a shop rag. He thanked me and wiped the oil from his hands. "We'll let it drain for a few minutes," he said as he tossed the rag to the ground. "Let's take five. Go grab us some water."

I headed for the refrigerator inside the garage. I'd taken about five steps when I heard Dad say, "Worthless piece-of-shit fucking Jeep."

Not looking back, I said "The Jeep heard that!"

"I know, I know!" Dad called after me. "Probably won't start again!"

I took bottles of water from the refrigerator and went back out to the driveway, handing a bottle to Dad. "It'd serve you right," I said with a wink.

I knew things used to be different for Dad, things I'd never been part of and would never know myself. It was not so much he became a changed person after losing Mom, more like an *adjusted* person. Whether Adjusted Dad was better or worse than Dad 1.0, I had no idea. It was a mystery I resigned myself to never being able to solve. I could remember images, Mom and Dad and me together, but they were only indistinct flashes like faded snapshots forever out-of-focus.

There was school and my friends. Rayven, Evie, and Cami. Uncle Vincent and Aunt Laurie. The town. My own hopes and dreams and confusions that seemed would never come together to make any sense. There was David Sills, Roger Gallo, and the rest of the gang I knew. There was old Checko and the Black Diamond Mine, but he and what he'd experienced were gone now. There was Casey Woodruff, always Casey Woodruff, infecting my thoughts like some arcane virus.

There was me and Dad, cleaning our own gutters, changing the oil in our one vehicle, cutting our grass, and doing every other task ourselves to maintain our home. While others in town hired out their yard work, took their vehicles to mechanics or paid an annual fee for furnace tune-ups, Dad and I were a self-contained maintenance shop, a DIY duo in our private kingdom, meager as it was. Not that our house was in any way run-down or sub-standard compared to other houses in town. It was well-kept with what Dad said was nice *curb appeal*. Our bills were always current. We were cool in the summer and warm in the winter. I was part of the free-lunch program at school, but so were a lot of my friends. My room had a comfortable bed, a nice desk, a closet to hang my clothes and a chest of drawers to store my socks and underwear. I had plenty of books, a PS5 gaming system, and a few games like Madden. I even had some choice action figures and accessories for Dungeons and Dragons, a tabletop role-playing game I'd discovered a year ago. As different as we may have been from our neighbors, we were the same. It was all relative. We could go out to eat whenever we wanted and often did—more than most of my friends. Things were different before I could remember, things like Dad. Things like Mom being alive. Other, unknown things. But this is what *I* knew and it was good and it was enough for me. I loved Dad and I knew he loved me. I was safe and had a home, a headquarters I could count on.

I was no different from you or anyone else.

I didn't miss what I didn't have.

———

Halfway through my Wendy's double-cheeseburger Dad told me from across the table The Strays were playing a two-night gig a hundred and twenty miles away in Vincennes over the weekend.

"That's cool!" I said through a mouthful of food. "*Wow!* Two nights!"

Dad's reaction was less than I expected. *Much* less.

He didn't react at all, save for pulling a deep drink from his straw and setting the obscenely large Wendy's drink cup aside and staring down at his food.

"That's great, Dad!" I tried again.

Only a slight nod from Dad, still studying his half-eaten burger. His fingers fished through the French fries, feeling for the most tender potato splinters. Dad hated overdone, crispy fries.

"*So...*" he started. He shook his head, slight and quick. It looked like some kind of involuntary tremor.

His face snapped up and he stared me in the face.

"You're going to spend the weekend with your aunt and uncle, at their house. I'll run you up there on Friday morning before I leave and be back to pick you up early Sunday afternoon."

"No problem, Dad."

His face was the face of a man who had just been found *Not Guilty* by a jury. His shoulders relaxed; the blood returned to his cheeks.

"No?"

"No, Dad," I answered. "It's cool. It's all good."

I went back to my double-cheeseburger and took a bite.

"You'll be fine," Dad said. "Your Aunt and Uncle, Rayven—they'll be there—"

"I know, Dad," I said between chewing a mouthful of hamburger, bun, and cheese. "Stay inside after dark."

"In the house or The Playhouse," Dad admonished.

I nodded, swallowing and taking a breath. "I got it, Dad. It's all good. I'll be fine."

"I know you'll be, son. You'll have a great time up there."

"Sure." I started fishing through my French fries, looking for perfection I knew waited somewhere in the pile of processed potatoes

61

stretched out on the greasy wrapper in front of me. I focused on that. I focused on me and Dad eating together at the table on a Tuesday evening. Less than three days later, I was going to spend not one, but *two* nights on top of Crumpton Hill at Uncle Vincent's house.

Brothers Vincent and John Baker had seen their dead parents there once, and not in a good way. Not in some phony John Edward and Long Island Medium reality-show TV way. According to Dad, Mom and Aunt Laurie had seen those spectral figures as well. What was about to happen? I wondered.

What would I see?

THE VINCENNES BREWING COMPANY
AND
ALVIS MUSIC
PROUDLY PRESENT
THE STRAYS
Finny Philchek—Lead Guitar, Vocals
Jack Cascio—Rhythm Guitar, Keyboard
Scott Watson—Bass
John Baker—Drums
TWO SHOWS: FRIDAY AND SATURDAY AT 9PM
ADVANCE TICKETS $10, AT THE DOOR $12
LIMITED CAPACITY, GET YOUR TICKETS NOW!

Above each name was a head shot of each member, their faces caught in various expressions on-stage from a past show.

Jack held the poster with both hands, staring at it like he was studying for the Bar Exam. Without warning, he said loudly from the back seat, "Finny looks like he's taking a shit!"

Everyone in the van burst into laughter. Jack nudged me in the ribs. "Whaddaya think, *Jules?* Grunting that solo right out!"

"Yeah, yeah," I said shyly, too afraid to join in the laughter.

"It's showmanship! I *am* the frontman!" Finny yelled back at him from the driver's seat.

Jack leaned forward with the poster. "See what it says here…The Strays. I don't see *The Philcheks anywhere.* Do you guys see *The Philcheks* on this poster?"

Finny slapped at the poster. "Hey, man, I'm drivin'."

In the front passenger seat, Dad took the poster from Jack. "It's one of the nicer ones. Better than what the Wine Garden did up for us."

On the other side of Jack, Scott grunted with disgust. "Boy, that's no shit," he agreed. "Why are me and John always listed last on these things?"

"You mean why is *John* listed last?" Finny asked.

"JOHN 'GINGER' BAKER AND THE THREE STOOGES!" Jack hollered loud enough to make me cringe.

Dad looked back at Jack. "I don't see that name here, either."

More laughter from everyone. The energy was high inside the van, a solid, confident feeling radiating from the guys. It suddenly occurred to me that it was almost like they were heading into a battle where there would be no danger, no casualties of war. A wave of nerves washed over me as we pulled into Uncle Vincent's driveway. I didn't want to do this anymore. I wished I was going the rest of the way to Vincennes with The Strays.

The van stopped and I sat there waiting for the engine to turn off. Time stood still. I looked over at Jack and Scott waiting frozen like mannequins. I looked at the back of Finny's unmoving head over the driver's seat. My eyes moved to the front passenger seat and there was Dad's face, turned back to me wearing a smile. The sight of him roused me from my waking dream. *Of course. The engine was still running because…*

"Here you are, son. Grab your stuff."

Nodding, I reached down and grabbed the bag at my feet, before twisting the latch and opening the sliding door.

"See ya, Jules," Jack said.

"Have a good time, Julie," Finny said.

"Have fun, Big J," Scott said.

I threw a wave over my shoulder as I stepped out. "Thanks, guys!" I answered in my cheeriest voice. It seemed to take all my strength to get the words out in that way.

Dad motioned me over from the open window of the passenger door. "See you on Sunday, first thing."

"Good show, Dad," I wished him.

"You know it, son," he said, putting his arm around the back of my neck and drawing me close enough to touch his forehead to mine. "Love you," he whispered.

"Love you, too, Dad," I whispered back.

Pulling his head back inside, I watched him face forward and raise an index finger at the windshield. The van rolled down the driveway and onto the asphalt. Finny honked the horn and I waved, watching the guys disappear down the desolate road.

Turning to the house, I heard a voice coming from inside.

An angry voice.

"NO!"

"No, I'm not going to calm down!"

"No, I'm not going to wait!"

"*You* explain it! I'm not doing this anymore! *I can't do it!*

The front door opened and Uncle Vincent appeared. He waved at me. I waved back and Aunt Laurie came through the door on his heels, side-stepping him and going straight to her car.

"Hi, Aunt Laurie," I called.

"Hi, Julian, the kids are excited to see you," she said, running the words together without looking at me. She got into the car and backed down the driveway. The rear tires spun with a squeal on the asphalt, leaving wisps of smoke in their wake. *Something was wrong.*

"Julian!" Uncle Vincent stood on the porch, arms outstretched, a painted smile on his face. Rather, a *pained* smile. Artificial, like the smile of a clown. Above that smile misted eyes betrayed a very different emotion. I could see he was trying his best to welcome me although I was there at a most inconvenient time and was anything *but* welcome. My stomach began to churn, my face going red hot as Uncle Vincent stepped off the porch and came up to me.

He didn't seem like the same person I'd encountered outside the Wine Garden a month ago. Or any other time for that matter. His strides were easy and informal. His clothes were not crisp and pressed, nor were they disheveled as much as casual. He just seemed...*like a regular person.*

He embraced me with both arms, holding me tight.

"It's good to have you, nephew. Good to see you," he said. "This is your house, too, all right? You make yourself at home." I thought I felt his body shudder a little, as if he were about to cry. I squeezed both my arms around the small of his back. It seemed like he needed it.

"Thanks, Uncle. Thank you."

He squeezed back, just for a second, then held me in front of him, his hands on my shoulders. "Look at you," he said.

He smiled for real this time, directly into my eyes. A smile meant just for me, deep and sincere. "You're a man, Julian. My God, it happened in a flash. I missed it!"

I didn't know how to respond to his heartfelt words. My strange Uncle Vincent had disappeared, replaced by just a guy.

"You sound like Dad," was all I could think to say.

He released me and shrugged. "Brothers. You know. Basically, the same."

Uncle Vincent jammed his hands into his pockets and looked around, as if trying to figure out what to say next.

"Rayven's out back—" he started, before Evie and Cami came running to us from the back yard, both of them yelling my name excitedly. "—and there you go," Uncle Vincent said with a flourish. "Your guides."

The twins almost crashed into us as they came to a stop. Cami grabbed my arm. "C'mon, c'mon!" she urged. "We're all out back!"

I heard Rayven before I saw him.

"Go out for a pass, chickenshit!"

Before I could yell, "Who you callin' a chickenshit?" Evie bolted away, screaming "Don't call her names!"

Rayven, holding a football, turned in our direction and brightened at seeing me. He launched the football. Before I could catch it, out of the corner of my eye, I saw Casey Woodruff, glaring at Rayven. Evie called Rayven an asshole as she ran by, Cami on her heels. The football hit the ground at my feet, bouncing perilously high. I lurched back to avoid a direct hit in the face. Coming up to me, Rayven flashed two thumbs up.

"Nice catch."

The three girls had disappeared inside The Playhouse.

My head was spinning. "What the hell, man?"

Rayven held a shrug. "What? It was right to you!"

I cuffed his chest. "I didn't know *she* was gonna be here."

Rayven picked up the football, tossing it from hand to hand. "All weekend, dude. The price I pay for having sisters, you know? You get to spend the weekend with me, they get to—"

"I got it, I got it," I said with a resigned nod.

A good nine hours until it got dark and I'd already started seeing disturbing things.

"Let's go hangout for a while at the pond," Rayven suggested.

"Got a hidden case of Falstaff there?" I joked.

Standing on the back deck of the house, Uncle Vincent called Rayven's name.

"What's up, Dad?"

"Let me borrow Julian for a second!"

"Okay!" Rayven answered. "I'll wait for you here," he said to me, offering no explanation.

I jogged across the grass up to the deck.

"Come on inside for a second."

"Sure, uncle."

I followed him into the house. Closing the French doors behind us, he put his arm over my shoulder, leading me through the kitchen into the living room where we sat down across from one another—him on a high-back chair with ornately-carved dark wood, me on a Victorian loveseat.

"You're not going to see your dead grandparents up here," he said, cutting right to the chase and betraying the fact that Dad had talked to him before talking to me. He flashed a smile before changing back into the Uncle Vincent I'd always known, without really changing. He was still wearing the loose-fitting casual clothes, the same face, but now he was skipping the chatter, speaking in the clipped and straight-forward way he always had before.

He leaned back in the chair, crossed his legs, and folded his hands in his lap. "But you still have to be inside before dark, like your cousins, like me and Aunt Laurie, same as everyone who stays here after the sun goes down. Things *do* come out at night up here, but they're in the yard, in the grass, sometimes they're up in the trees. Nobody knows why it happens or what exactly comes out and wanders around. It's not like a movie. You can't look out the windows and watch monsters cavorting over the lawn or beating on the door trying to get inside. There's nothing outside after dark that can hurt you. You just have to be inside once the sun goes down. Anywhere in here or in The Playhouse."

"If I *do* go outside, what happens?"

Uncle Vincent shook his head. "Don't go outside. Don't leave The Playhouse. Period. You understand me?"

I swallowed hard. "Yes, sir."

Uncle Vincent uncrossed his legs and leaned forward, his clasped hands resting on his knees. "And now I'm going to tell you something your dad couldn't."

I felt suddenly afraid and like I was about to cry. But Uncle Vincent smiled at me for the second time in my life.

"Everyone loved your mother, Julian. Even your grandparents, both of whom you've already heard weren't exactly the best mother and father to me and your dad. Michelle had a way about her. A quality that people couldn't help but like. She brought people together just by her presence. When she got sick, when she passed, everyone who knew her was devastated. It was so sudden; she was so young…" and bowed his head. When he looked up again, his eyes were cloudy with sorrow. "She was the best of us." He sighed. "After she was gone, your dad and I agreed to keep you away from here after dark. In case you might see her…*here*."

It was too much to hear. I didn't know how to feel, how to react.

67

"Have you seen her? Has Rayven or…or…*has anyone ever seen her?*"

"No, son. No, we haven't. But it may be different for you. I'm telling you now, don't look for her. You may not like what you see."

Uncle Vincent stood up. Our conversation was over.

———————

The pond atop Crumpton Hill was an anomaly as far as ponds go. Formed after the collapse of the Black Diamond Mine it grew from little more than a puddle to a calm body of water an acre across until its natural expansion came to a halt. People in Harris and Rosedale said the water bubbled up from the mine after the failed attempt to rescue all but Checko Muciarelli, using hoses on full blast from fire trucks in both towns in the hope that the miners would float up to the surface on a cushion of water unharmed. But I knew better from Checko himself. There had been no such rescue attempt. No water from firetruck hoses or anywhere else. Checko had been pulled from the collapsed mine from a dry hole alongside the ruined elevator shaft dug by countless volunteers and bucket-cranes where the pond now sat, still waters hosting fish and croaking frogs. Why it remained a vibrant pool of constantly fresh oxygen-rich water capable of sustaining marine life when it should have been a stagnant body of dead swamp water? No one dared ask. And so, the people of Harris and Rosedale ignored the pond on top of Crumpton Hill. When ownership passed to Vincent and Laurie Baker, everyone forgot about it altogether. It was a mile down a walking trail from the edge of the backyard, just behind The Playhouse. Halfway down the trail, after trading small talk and the usual good-natured insults with Rayven, I gave voice, clumsy as it was, to the exchange between my aunt and uncle I'd witnessed coming out of the van.

"Where'd Aunt Laurie go? She left right after Dad dropped me off."

"Mom left, huh?" Rayven asked as if it was no big deal.

"Yeah. I saw her take off in the Camaro."

"*Eh.*"

"What?"

"They fight all the time."

"All the time?" I asked with surprise. "What about?"

"Almost there," was all he said.

The pond was a sight to behold. Nestled in a clearing surrounded by endlessly tall narrow evergreens, sunlight glistening off the water, it was like something artificial, constructed for a movie set. It was beautiful.

Taking up a place on the bank at the edge of the water, Rayven cursed under his breath. "*Damn.* Shoulda brought a couple of fishing poles."

I sat down beside him and gathered my knees to my chest. "We can come back tomorrow and do some fishing," I offered.

"I don't know…" Rayven said, his voice trailing off softly.

Still focused on the fishing, I said, "Won't be a problem."

Without warning, Rayven said, "They're gonna get divorced. I don't know. Mom can't take the way things are, I mean, the way things have always been up here. She just can't take it anymore." He started to cry but laughed instead. "Dad," he said. "I don't know, man, you know?"

Having no idea what to say, I scooted across the ground closer to him until our legs were touching as Rayven continued.

"I mean, I get it, you know? *Can't go out at night* and all that shit, but it's *real*, you know? You *can't* go out at night unless you want to walk through a fucking waking nightmare. I get why Mom's tired of this shit. But I get why Dad's like, 'This is our home; it's okay. I love you. It's all bugs and spiders as long the family stays together.' I get what they're both saying, you know? What I don't get is how they can both be right and still hate each other."

"They don't hate each other," I heard myself say. "Something more is going on. Have *you* ever seen anything? What about Evie and Cami?"

"Sure, I have." He rolled his eyes. "You think I've lived my whole life hearing *Don't go outside after dark* without ever going outside after dark?"

"I'm sorry, I'm just trying to figure—"

"My fault. I'm sorry, bro. I didn't mean to snap, you know? Hell, this is your first night here. I've spent sixteen years on this hill."

"What have you seen?"

"Things," Rayven answered. "Animals I thought were rabbits or a dog until they got closer and I could tell they were *things* instead, like made-up animals that don't exist. The rabbit would have horns in place of ears. Once I saw what looked like a cat at my feet. When I bent down, I saw it had centipede legs." He finished with a shrug. "*Weird shit.*"

The casualness of his tone was startling and left me with a lingering feeling of unease. What he said next sent a chill up the back of my neck.

"You won't see those things. You'll see something different if you're the only one looking."

I heard Dad's words ringing inside my head. *I'd have to see for myself.*

We explored the banks of the pond for the next couple hours mostly in silence, each of us lost in our own private thoughts.

Knowing I was the only person who hadn't experienced what every other person closest to me had made me feel like an outcast or initiate for membership in some long-established club. Hours earlier, when there had been intimacy between me and my own small circle of people whom I loved, now I felt detached from those I'd once counted on. I felt isolated from them all, completely alone. I was frightened but the fear was warm and almost soothing as it grew.

I could only imagine what Rayven was going through. His torment over the situation between his mom and dad was palpable. No wonder he'd described the night terrors he'd encountered outside the house in such mundane terms, as one would describe a trip to the grocery store. I missed my mother but could barely remember her. Still, I would face the Devil himself without thinking twice if it would bring her back. For my cousin and best friend, the prospect of his parents divorcing at this point in his life, when he was inches away from coming into his own yet stuck in the *In-Between Time* of high school and all that included had to be a terror beyond belief. Certainly, more than living with any animals, ghosts, or monsters unable to enter buildings and forced to roam only under night skies.

It was a little before two in the afternoon when we came off the trail, emerging from the trees into the backyard.

A little less than six hours before sundown.

———————

The backyard was deserted. No sign of the twins, which was a good thing because it meant no sign of Casey Woodruff.

Uncle Vincent appeared at The Playhouse door and saw us coming across the yard. Waving us over, we joined him.

"Thought I'd order five or six pizzas for everyone," he said. Stepping back inside The Playhouse, we followed him.

There was a long table set up off to one side. There were plastic cups; two-liter bottles of Coke, Sprite and Dad's Root Beer; napkins and paper plates on top of the table. Underneath was a cooler filled with ice. We nodded our approval to Uncle Vincent.

The Playhouse was cordoned off; the back half hidden by several tri-fold partitions while the front half was filled with floor pillows and a few sleeping bags. There was a PlayStation connected to a 40-inch television. A dozen action figures of G.I. Joes and Johhny West cowboys and several copies of *Famous Monsters of Filmland* and other monster magazines were scattered about the floor. Two large beanbag seats were in front of the television.

"I wanted to ask all of you guys together, but you were at the pond. The girls chose here. You guys can stay here, too, or in the house." A thin smile crossed Uncle Vincent's face. "I'm sure the pizza will taste the same wherever you decide to stay."

"The Playhouse is great," I heard myself say before I could think. *Damn it.*

"Sure, Dad. That way we won't be juggling pizzas from here to the house."

Uncle Vincent regarded the table with pride. "All settled then," he declared. "I'll order the pizzas around five. The girls already told me what they wanted. How 'bout you guys?"

71

"Cheese pizza with extra cheese, half-portion of sauce…and an order of cheesy garlic bread."

"Your usual," Uncle Vincent said to Rayven.

"Double mushrooms and pepperoni, extra cheese and half-sauce," I said. "And cheesy garlic bread."

Uncle Vincent winked. "You got it, Julian." He pointed to my bag on the floor next to the table. "You left that in the yard. I took the liberty."

I blushed. I'd completely forgotten about it. I opened my mouth to apologize, but Uncle Vincent shook his hand at me and winked again. With that he left The Playhouse.

Expecting Rayven to admonish me for choosing to spend the night in the same place with his sisters and their friend, I braced myself to be dressed down. Instead, he gave me the grand tour of his space which, at least for the next two nights, would be *our* space. Even though I'd seen the place before on days Dad and I visited, he was a gleeful tour guide, giddy as he pointed out every amenity. I understood his excitement. Slumber parties were commonplace to his sisters but as far as I knew, I was Rayven's first overnight guest.

Instead of pointing out that I'd seen The Playhouse less than two months ago, I let him go on about the latest issue of *Monster Bash:* "Over there next to my sleeping bag, great Vincent Price Tribute issue," and a couple of new action figures he pointed out: "propped up against the wall over there."

From where we stood: Two G.I. Joe soldiers, mean-looking brutes, their square-jawed stern faces scowling out from under fuzzy crew-cuts.

His mania was infectious. "*Very* cool!" I exclaimed. "What's new up in your room?"

"Nothing much," he said, growing suddenly calm. "We'd have a bathroom to ourselves if we stayed there tonight." It was not so much the admonishment I expected, but in his own way he was calling me out just the same.

I tried to redeem myself. "We can stay at the house; it really doesn't matter to me."

72

Rayven paraphrased the rationale he'd given his dad minutes before. "No, this is perfect, bro. Better to eat hot pizza here than battling my sisters and then carrying it all the way up to my room."

"You're right. Okay."

"I thought you might be freaked out by Woodruff being here, you know."

I played dumb. "*Woodruff? Oh, you mean Casey? Yeah, no.* I mean, no, no. I hadn't even thought that."

Rayven seemed to see through my act. He squinted at me with a sly smile. "Okay, *killer.* It's cool."

Was I *so* easy to see through?

I wanted to tell him to *STFU*, and I would've, too.

Except he was right.

"Whoa!" Rayven said, stooping to pick up a G.I. Joe lying in the grass outside The Playhouse. He tossed it through The Playhouse opening. "Can't leave that out. Getting dark."

———————

The pizza delivery arrived a little after six.

Uncle Vincent finished what he'd started, playing steward and waiter. He arranged the pizza boxes and cartons of hot garlic cheese bread in neat rows down the table, carefully spacing the boxes just so, buffet-style. After exclaiming, "Oldest First!" he slapped three slices on his paper plate and grabbed a single napkin. He took no bread or drink as he left, bidding us "Goodnight" and "Have fun." I watched him walk across the yard and disappear into the house as twilight cast a bright yellow glow over the yard.

Everyone gorged themselves on the food, coming back for seconds and thirds.

Rayven and I played *Battleship* while we ate. The girls did whatever they were doing in their space behind the partition, a million miles away at the rear half of the vast Quonset hut. During our reveries, twilight passed into night unnoticed.

Yanking the joystick on my controller, I shouted at the TV screen as my character took a fatal blow.

"Oh! You *BASTARD! SONOFABITCH!*"

The words echoed over the still of the room. My head still in the game, I turned to Rayven and yelled, "WHAT THE FU — ?"stopping in mid-fuck.

Rayven was sprawled over the bean bag chair, controller still in hand, fast asleep. I regarded him for one, maybe two entire minutes. Yep. He was out. Now, my movements were quiet and slow, not wanting to wake him up. I rose from the beanbag chair and turned the TV volume down before closing the game. There was no sound from the partition behind us, no sign of lights or life. The girls, I reasoned, must be asleep as well.

I shut off the small lamp on the floor beside the TV and returned to the beanbag. There on the floor next to me sat the TV remote. Picking it up, I hit the INFO button.

The top right of the screen displayed the time: 10:54pm.

I was less than two feet away from the entrance of The Playhouse — the "front door" which was a ten-foot-high transparent tarp made of thick-mil plastic split down the middle. There was no lock to work, no hinges to creak. One had only to pass through the split to the yard.

I looked over at Rayven's sleeping form.

Turning back to the partition, I listened for any sign of activity, watching for a light to come on. There was nothing. No sounds, no movement, no lights. Everyone was asleep. I stood up again, holding my breath.

I looked through the tarp into the shadows over the yard, studying the blades of dull green grass standing at attention under the moonlight.

Exhaling a torrent of breath, I stepped outside.

My eyes pinballed left and right, up and down, hyper-vigilant. Pushing forward into the middle of the yard with raised forearms and expectant fingers ready to close into fists at a moment's notice, I braced myself for anything.

A high breeze rustled the treetops, making me flinch. It passed as quickly as it came, leaving me to exhale in relief.

Passing under a faint light glow from a single upstairs window of the house I recognized it as coming from the second-floor bathroom. *A plug-in nightlight.*

I walked to the tree line and waited. Then I wondered what I was waiting for. Some kind of monster? *Really?* Some kind of animal that was not an animal? A dog with a buffalo head? What *was* it I was waiting for and why did I think there was something *worth* waiting for at all?

I turned from the trees, walked into the middle of the yard, and sat down on the grass. There were fools and then there was me. The ultimate punchline to a private joke.

I stared at The Playhouse, expecting Rayven and his sisters to burst through the tarp pointing and laughing at me. Casey Woodruff would come out and give me a running kick in the balls for an encore and everyone would have a good laugh at the stupid guy who lost the game because he didn't know the rules.

When that didn't happen, I closed my eyes and thought about my mother. I thought about all the wisdom she must have held, lost to time and circumstances out of anyone's control that she'd never be able to give to me. Instead, I was left with a father who didn't seem to know or refused to share what he knew about what Michelle Baker desired to pass on to her son. I was left with a creepy uncle and a cousin who talked in riddles at my expense. Truth to tell, the bottom line was they *all* talked to me in riddles.

I grew angrier the longer I sat in the grass. The ass of my jeans went cold and wet, soaked through with dew. Cursing, I stood up and marched back into The Playhouse. Kicking off my shoes, I turned to the tarp "front door," opening the slit wide and clearing my throat. With raging disdain, I launched a gob of spit over the yard.

Things come out at night my ass.

A loud belch erupted from the bottom of my stomach. The recycled taste of mushroom and pepperoni and garlic burned my nostrils. My head felt like a brick, my stomach heavy with the doughy meal we'd all gorged on. No wonder everyone was asleep. I was tired myself. I swooned back and forth, ready to pass out. I had the presence of mind to lay myself down on the sleeping bag to avoid a free-fall. Within seconds, I was asleep.

———

I woke a few minutes past two in the morning.

It took a few seconds to get my bearings. I blinked twice to focus my eyes. Rayven was curled into the beanbag a few feet away, his faint snores rattling over the otherwise silent space. I shivered, groping for a blanket but finding nothing. Raising my head to look around, my eyes fixed on the tarp and the yard beyond.

Something was dancing back and forth on the grass.

Something.

Blinking again, I craned my head toward the tarp.

It was a pale blob of an object. Not dancing. *Bouncing.*

A self-contained round glob without arms or legs, lurching toward The Playhouse. It flopped over the grass like a living fistful of Play-Doh. Its features were indistinct until it got closer and I could see there was a face.

Eyes of solid black circles fixed me in a stare as the thing came right up to the outside of the tarp. The clear plastic pushed inward as the bulbous and crooked nose contacted the tarp and stopped. I felt my body stretched out on the sleeping bag, propped up by my elbows as my own face, twice the size of the grotesque visage, stared back into the coal-black maws of the creature's lifeless eyes.

The mouth was a jagged line, as if carved by a seismograph needle. I watched the distorted nostrils heave in and out with unnatural breath. My own breath hitched deep in my throat, refusing to come out as I waited for the incomprehensible devastation I was sure to come at any second.

This was not dead grandparents.

Not a cat with centipede legs.

This was something never seen before.

Something special sent from Hell.

Just for me.

I opened my mouth to scream but couldn't make a sound.

The thing was inches away and only separated from my face by a twelve-foot clear tarp with an eight-foot slit down the middle. It rocked slowly back and forth, staring at me with a blank expression.

And then, the mouth-slit opened wide, pushing the nose upward. The shape of its head reacted by pulsating with tumorous lumps rising and falling and rising again as the thing spoke.

The first word came out like the slow peal of a foghorn.

Frollo

The second word was higher pitched, each syllable articulated with precise pronunciation.

Chess-Ter-Ton

And the third, a solemn moan.

Moldern

The face rattled against the tarp, repeating the gibberish faster.

Frollo...Chess-Ter-Ton...Moldern

I cocked my arm back, ready to throw a punch toward the tarp, hoping to send the mishappen visage anywhere but within inches of where I lay. Before I could launch my assault, I saw the G.I. Joe figure and picked it up. I meant to thrust my hand forward to waggle the G.I. Joe at the thing, hoping it would be scared away.

Instead, my hand went too far forward, pushing through the slit in the tarp to the outside.

Two things happened at once.

The Play-Doh thing vanished.

And the twelve-inch G.I. Joe clenched in my fist began to struggle under my grip. When it saw me, its jaw dropped and it froze.

Then it screamed.

Then I screamed.

G.I. Joe started to beat his tiny hands against my closed fist. Yanking my arm back inside The Playhouse, my body began thrashing as I kicked my feet and slapped my hands over my face and chest, eyes squeezed shut. At some point, I let go of G.I. Joe. When I opened my eyes, he was sprawled across one of the monster magazines, an inanimate action figure once again.

I felt a hard punch on my shoulder blade and there was Casey Woodruff alongside me. "*Stupid!*" she said, thrusting her index finger at the tarp entrance. "You knocked it outside!"

I looked between the split in the tarp to the yard beyond.

Outside The Playhouse, feet planted firmly in the grass, the 12-inch figure of Johhny West stared in at us, his little plastic gun pointed squarely at Casey and me.

Glowering at us, the little cowboy said in a squeaky voice, "Where's my Janie, you bushwhackers?"

Casey pushed forward off my shoulder, thrusting her arm through the tarp and grabbing Jonny West by his tiny vinyl head.

There was a sharp *crack!* like one of those Snap-N-Pops we threw on the cement every Independence Day while we waited for the proper fireworks.

Casey yelped in pain, throwing Johnny West behind her. The cowboy action figure landed next to his plastic wife, Jane, and was still.

We both scooted backward into The Playhouse, putting a safe distance between us and the opening of the tarp.

"*Jesus Christ!* I figured everyone was asleep. *Holy shit*, I don't believe this. An action figure, for God's sake."

"Everyone *is* asleep," Casey Woodruff said, glaring at me with a mix of anger and pain. "What happened happened and now it's over."

Before she could move away from me, I took her hand in mine.

A thin trickle of blood ran down the inside of her forearm.

"You're hurt."

"Johnny shot me," Casey said, her voice softer. "It's nothing. Felt like a bee sting."

She tried to pull away, but I held her fast. Looking around, I found a napkin from our pizza party lying on the floor. I picked it up and dabbed the wound, no bigger than a pinhead. "I'm so sorry. It was all my fault. I didn't know."

Her arm relaxed as I tended to the injury. Wiping the blood away, I saw a dot no bigger than the head of a pin under the skin. "I am so sorry, Casey." The bleeding had stopped, leaving only the graphite-colored dot. I rubbed my finger gently over it. "I don't feel anything. I think it's okay. Does it hurt?"

She put her hand over mine. Her fingers were soft like feathers, I thought, softer than anything in the whole wide world.

She leaned into me; her face so close to mine I could feel her warm, sweet-smelling breath.

"Thank you," she said. "I'm okay. Let's go to sleep now and I'll see you in the morning."

PART TWO

Dark Places

Chapter Eight

The Lighted Man

Wrapped in the sleeping bag, I woke easily to the sounds of a video game in progress. Eyes closed, I listened to the back and forth of the game and the voices of Rayven and Evie.

After calling Rayven an *asshole* yesterday after he'd teased Casey with his *chickenshit* comment, Evie hadn't so much as looked at her brother the rest of the day, much less talked to either one of us during our pizza party for the rest of the night. Now, brother and sister were warring in a more innocuous way: through a screen, their real-life enmity forgotten.

I opened one eye to confirm what I was hearing.

There they were, Rayven and Evie Baker, sitting side-by-side, controllers in hand. They were laughing and yelling together, enjoying the game despite its frustrations.

Evie and Cami were fewer than two years apart in age from me and Rayven. I'm guessing here, but it's almost like Uncle Vincent and Aunt Laurie decided they wanted a certain number of kids and wanted to get it out of the way as fast as possible. Whether they counted on twins after their second and last successful attempt, I do not know.

Evie was an outspoken fireball. A Type-A extrovert if ever there was. Suffering no fools, nor what she perceived as fools, Evie took no prisoners from elementary school into junior high.

On the playground:

Evie was often left with ripped clothes and a dirty face, her tears turning to mud as they rolled down her cheeks. On the other hand, her opponents were left on the ground with bloodied noses, screaming for a teacher and ready to tattle their version of the account to any adult who would listen. Evie stood her ground against bullies, always giving back better than her attackers could. The schism between the adult world and childhood world being what it's always been would turn Evie from the bullied to the bully when grown-ups got involved. But Evie never cared. She had a strong sense of right and wrong and was a stalwart character from an early age. She didn't like bullies and that was that.

In the first year of high school:

Evie was suspended for two weeks after receiving a *"D"* grade on her essay regarding the novel *Tom Sawyer*. She launched into a tirade in front of the class on how Mark Twain *had* to have been either drunk or on drugs when he wrote what she characterized as "this piece of shit," concluding by calling her English I teacher a *cocksucker*.

Cami was very different. Even though they were twins—in the birth-timeline at least—Cami was the polar opposite of Evie. She was introspective, more given to thought than action and generally regarded by everyone as shy.

On the playground:

Cami loved to swing if the swing set was empty. She would avoid the activity if any of her classmates were swinging. Even if there was a vacant seat. Instead, she would walk the fence line of the schoolyard in solitude, her feet shuffling along the grass until recess ended. Sometimes she would pick a fallen branch off the ground and carry it with her, talking to it as if the dead stick was a kindred spirit.

In the first year of high school:

Every one of Cami's teachers characterized her as "gifted," at the same time mis-characterizing her shyness as "immaturity." Their conclusion was a wishy-washy position of *not quite ready* for so-called "advanced classes," which suited Cami fine. She was comfortable in her skin. She knew what she knew and she knew it better than anyone. Certainly, better than any teacher whom she felt had only a temporary interest in her as a person. She didn't think her teachers truly cared about whether she learned anything or not. She consulted the one person she knew she could trust. Her twin sister, Evie.

"Buncha' dicks," Evie advised. "If they give you any shit, punch 'em in the goddamn throat." Evie pointed at the middle of her neck. "Right here. *Hard.*"

Cami loved her sister but decided to remain skeptical of her advice.

"Hey, cousin," Evie said. She'd looked behind her and noticed I was awake before I could feign sleep again. I raised my head from the sleeping bag and offered a good morning to her. Rayven was leaning so far forward at the TV screen, fingers working his controller like playing a jazz piano, he looked as if would collapse on his face any second.

"Yeah, yeah! I *got* your ass—*WHAT THE HELL?!*" Rayven flinched to one side as Evie's controller bounced off his head.

"Game's over," Evie said. She went through the tarp and was gone.

"*Hey!*" Rayven yelled at her.

"Morning," I said to him.

Rayven rubbed his head. "Man, that *hurt*," he said, frowning with pain as I pulled myself from the sleeping bag. He searched the floor around him for the controller. "If she broke it—"

"You'll have to use one of your other three," I said brightly.

Rayven grunted. "*Sisters.* Be glad you're an only child."

Be glad your mother's still alive, you prick.

The thought came from nowhere for no reason I could explain. It was angry, mean-spirited, and meant to do nothing but lash out and hurt Rayven. I was grateful for whatever self-restraint I possessed that I hadn't said it out loud.

"What were you guys playing?" I said instead.

"Halo." Rayven sighed, searching the floor for Evie's controller, still muttering "…if it's broke…I *swear*…"

The girls came through the tarp into The Playhouse.

"Want a re-match?" Evie asked Rayven with a snide grin as she walked by.

"Stupid video games always win anyway," Cami offered.

"Halo." Casey Woodruff declared, bringing up the rear behind the twins. As the three girls passed us on their way to their space at the back of The Playhouse, Casey shot me a glance before saying to Rayven, "I think messing with action figures is your cousin's game."

My shoulders sank at the words. I watched her follow the twins with a nonchalant strut, trying to think of a clever response to redeem myself. My mouth fell open, but nothing came out.

"Julian *owns* those G.I. Joes," she called to no one without turning around. I didn't know whether to feel pride or humiliation. I think I felt a little of both.

Even with her back to me as she walked away, I was transfixed by Casey Woodruff.

"Go pound sand!" Rayven hollered at them. "*Snotty brats.*"

He turned to me, proud of himself as if to say, *Take that!*

"Yeah," I agreed weakly. "Good one."

Rayven asked if I'd slept well. "Perfect," I lied.

"Let's hit the pond and do some fishing while it's still early," he blurted out of nowhere. The Halo game forgotten, Rayven slapped the tarp aside and bounded over the dew-covered grass. "Everything's ready!" I heard him yell as I sat there, watching the abandoned TV screen go from the game to a screensaver. The design floated from top to bottom and all around as I stood and followed Rayven's voice.

The morning passed quickly at the pond. I didn't say a thing about what I'd seen the night before and Rayven never asked. If I'd told him about the floating Play-Doh head and G.I. Joe and Johnny West figure coming to life, not to mention whatever the hell the *Frollo-moldering* gibberish meant, I knew he'd only answer with other questions like "Who knows?" or "What do you think?" or some such other horseshit. Forget mentioning Casey Woodruff.

When we weren't staring transfixed at our lines, taut over the still water and waiting for any telltale jerk of the poles, we talked about the best ways to catch fish, trading our individual techniques. By lunchtime, we returned to the house with two stringers of keepers, plump largemouth bass between two and four pounds each, although I will swear to this day that I had a five-pound big mouth on my stringer. Fish tales aside, between the two of us, we had more than enough for a decent fish-fry, enough to feed me and Rayven, Evie, Cami, and Casey, Uncle Vincent and —

Aunt Laurie.

I saw her as we came off the path into the backyard.

Smiling and waving, Uncle Vincent at her side, she hollered a greeting to us.

Reaching the deck, we dropped the stringers of fish, heaving to catch our breath. Aunt Laurie turned to Uncle Vincent and kissed his cheek. "Well." She studied the dozen flopping and gasping fish at her feet. "I'll make the French fries."

"In the meantime, there's leftover pizza for lunch," Uncle Vincent offered.

"The girls have already had potato salad and ham sandwiches," Aunt Laurie added.

Rayven was buoyed by his mom's presence. "We'll get these cleaned right away. They'll be ready for supper, *promise.*"

Uncle Vincent beamed at us. "I'll make sure the grill is fired up."

"It'll be great!" Rayven exclaimed. "A fish fry!"

And it was great. A memory I'll never forget.

Uncle Vincent manned the grill, frying our fish along with hot dogs and hamburgers.

Everyone was laughing around the picnic table as we ate. Rayven was as animated as a high-def cartoon character, trading jokes with his sisters and me as he switched from gulping mouthfuls of fish to devouring at least three hot dogs. Uncle Vincent and Aunt Laurie sat conspicuously close to one another, whispering ear to ear then giggling. Casey launched a chunk of potato salad in my direction from across the table, using her plastic fork as a catapult. It landed squarely in the puddle of baked beans on my plate. She put a hand over her mouth to conceal her delight as I feigned indignation with an exaggerated glare. We locked our eyes for longer than necessary, neither one of us willing to look away. I think both of us were trying to figure out what the hell was going on.

The day grew dim. One-by-one, we stood up and began to clear the picnic table. First, Uncle Vincent. Then Aunt Laurie gestured to the girls to follow her lead. We cleaned the picnic table, throwing our cups and paper plates into a big Rubbermaid trash barrel alongside the backyard deck. All of us were still talking back and forth, yelling to no one in particular about the great food and how full we were and how perfect everything had been.

I dumped my cup, paper plate, plastic knife and fork and handful of crumpled napkins into the trash barrel when I looked up at the deck and saw Rayven standing next to his parents.

Night was falling.

Rayven stabbed a thumb over his shoulder. "I'm gonna sleep inside tonight, dude."

I raised my right hand, giving him the rock-and-roll devil horns with my index and pinkie fingers. I didn't feel slighted that he hadn't asked me to join him. I knew he didn't want to hurt my feelings. He knew it, too. Sure, we were cousins, but that didn't matter.

We had grown up together, been friends long enough to understand what the other meant by a glance or gesture. Tonight, Rayven wanted to be as close to his parents as possible. He felt a change coming, telling me as much as the day before at the pond. He wanted to hang on to what he knew as long as he could. He wanted to spend time in the same place as his mom and dad while there was still time. I held the devil horns high above my head as I turned away from the deck and trotted toward The Playhouse, hearing the laughter of the girls from somewhere deep inside.

All I wanted to do was go to sleep. That was my plan.

———————

Evie and Casey were in the middle of some video game three feet away from my sleeping bag. Ignoring them, I went to the sleeping bag and saw a few magazines scattered nearby. Grabbing a copy of *Monster Bash*, I knelt next to the bag and pulled the flap open, jumping to my feet with a startled yelp.

"*BOO!*" Casey shouted at the same time I saw the G.I. Joe lying on his back where my head would be, little plastic arms posed as if reaching up to grab me.

My face turned red at the sound of the two of them laughing at their perfect set-up.

I couldn't help but nod my head, saying with a defeated smile, "That's beautiful. Come up with that all by yourselves, did you?"

"Yeah, we did," Evie said between her fits of giggling. "And you thought *you* caught the biggest fish today! Shoulda seen your face!"

"I know, I know." I had to admit it. Casey leaned back slightly so Evie couldn't see her mouth the word "sorry" through her smile. With a thumbs-up meant to signal Casey more than anything else, I said "You got me, ladies."

"Let's watch a movie; you wanna watch a movie?" Evie demanded and asked Casey in a single sprint of words. She pushed her knees off the floor and, without waiting for an answer, ran across the floor behind the partition. "I'll go pick something!"

I turned back to meet Casey's stare. "*That wasn't funny,*" I hissed, glaring at her. "*Does she know what that was about?*"

Casey shook her head.

"I must have looked like an idiot. Everyone must think I'm some kind of fool."

Casey shook her head again. She scooted her knees closer to me, keeping her voice low as she spoke. "No. I wouldn't do that to you. Nobody else knows what happened last night."

She looked toward the partition. She started to rise, stopping. "I gotta go. I'll try to come back out after everyone goes to sleep. We can talk then." She paused with a hopeful expression. "Okay?"

"Okay."

"Okay." She scrambled to her feet and trotted away. As she was halfway across The Playhouse, Evie poked her head out from behind the partition, two DVDs in her hand.

"*School of Rock* or *Fifty First Dates*?"

———————

I paged through a few magazines and read the two latest issues of *Black Hammer* comic books before my eyelids grew heavy and my vision blurred. Pulling myself into the sleeping bag and shuffling around to find that perfect comfy spot, my body relaxed and I closed my eyes. The last sound I heard was the toilet flush from the half-bath at the very rear of The Playhouse as I wondered which movie they had decided to watch.

A vague dream of being pinned down rolled over me like a slow wave. I came awake, still frozen inside the sleeping bag as the dream crested and rolled back, retreating from my dawning consciousness. Groggy, but awake nevertheless, I held my breath, aware of a pressure on my back outside the sleeping bag running the length of my body. Opening one eye, I could see long delicate fingers curled over my shoulder. Exhaling a gust of breath, I shifted my legs against a pair of other legs on the outside of the sleeping bag.

"Julian," Casey whispered in my ear. "Are you awake?"

I blew another deep breath. "I am now. How's your arm?"

"It's okay," she continued to whisper, the words blowing a warm breeze into my ear. "I didn't want to wake you."

I stifled a laugh. "But giving me a heart attack was okay."

"What?"

"I said 'Giving me—'"

"Julian—"

"What?"

Casey's cheek was pressed again mine, her whispers moving over the side of my face now.

"Thanks for asking about my arm."

Her hand found mine, our palms pressed together. My fingers intertwined with hers.

"You're holding my hand," I said trying to sound annoyed.

"I am," she whispered.

"Okay," I whispered back.

Our hands squeezed tighter together. I felt us relax at the same time. Minutes passed in silence as I watched the unmoving magazines in my line of vision, feeling the rhythm of Casey breathing against my back, the pillow of her cheek against mine, the clutch of our hands. Maybe I should have been trying to figure out what was happening. And by that, I mean with my dad, with Uncle Vincent and Aunt Laurie, with their house, with things roaming outside at night here on top of Crumpton Hill, with my own life. Maybe I should have been using the time to figure all of that out, or to at least think about it. But I didn't use the time for that and I didn't care. For those fleeting moments all that mattered was how good it felt to share a quiet and pure connection with Casey Woodruff without the confusion of pre-conceived biases or the overall chaos by which my life seemed to be defined.

Creepy Casey.

The name rang sour in my head for the first time. Maybe I'd figured out one thing after all. But who could say?

For the next two hours, we kneeled together face to face and talked about what we'd seen. Casey did most of the talking since she'd spent nights up here off and on for the last two years while I had seen a Play-Doh head and a toy come to life. It took me five minutes to bring her up to speed on what I'd seen so far and I'd left out the fact that the Play-Doh head had spoken to me. I'd left out the gibbering moan *Frollo Chess-Ter-Ton Moldern.*

On Casey's first overnight visit, she was thirteen years old and saw a battle between feral winged squirrels and giant black widow spiders in the trees. The battle spilled onto the ground and the spiders swarmed up the outside of the tarp in retreat, turning the two sheets of clear plastic into a single black velvet entity, squirming with the beat of a thousand tapping legs and bulbous bodies. Since then, she had seen a funeral procession moving across the yard, two groups of pallbearers carrying dual caskets with the names of her parents emblazoned on each. She'd seen herself commit suicide by hanging from the railing of the backyard deck. She'd watched as hundreds of slugs arched and slid over the grass, all wearing the face of her puppy, Fred, who'd died of Parvo three days after Christmas when she was nine years old.

Evie and Cami had tried to warn her in the same familiar way as Rayven, Dad, and Uncle Vincent tried to warn me; a vague "you'll see for yourself" introduction to the horrors limited only by the number of people who witnessed them.

"Oh," was all I could say as I understood what my sudden realization implied. "Oh," I repeated. What must Rayven have seen for all these years? What must he be seeing now? As for Evie and Cami…

"Cami sees a lot of bugs. Not real bugs, you know, stuff like flying fish-head bugs or crickets walking on the grass with human legs and chirping in human voices."

I started to hyperventilate.

"Evie, now *Evie* has seen some *really* scary shit. Mostly, it's always been the same for her: Strangers screaming into the tarp about how she let them down, how they trusted her and she let them down. She was the last one to see things, I mean after me and Cami. She gave us endless shit for a long time. She thought we were nuts. She even slapped Cami after Cami told her she'd seen a bumble bee the size of a crow wearing a helmet and buzzing over the yard. Evie slapped her so hard that Cami pissed her pants. Your Aunt drove me back home that night, ending our slumber party before it even started. She told my parents that Evie was to blame, that I was always welcome back, but she was bringing me back home to punish Evie for what she did to Cami. That was early on, you know? At this point, Evie is more scared of what's out there than either me or Cami."

I turned away and gasped into my fist until I could breathe once more. How could Casey be telling me about these things with such calm, so casually as if what she was saying was anything close to normal? Anger welled up inside me. Why did Uncle Vincent and Aunt Laurie stay here? Why did they embrace such an absolute nightmare after all these years? Selling the house and getting the hell off

Crumpton Hill seemed like a no-brainer anyone else would have gladly embraced given these circumstances.

"The action figures," I mumbled. "We *both* saw the action figures. We both saw the same thing."

"We did," Casey agreed. She took both my hands in hers. "We were looking at the same time."

That made sense. She hadn't seen Play-Doh head and so far, it hadn't reappeared. In fact, outside the tarp, I saw nothing but the lawn and the house beyond.

"I was with Evie the night she came around; the first time she knew Cami and I were telling the truth. It was a month later, the first time I'd been allowed to come back and spend the night. It was uncomfortable at first, but we all settled into the way we were before Evie slapped the piss out of Cami."

Casey laughed at what she'd just said. "*Literally.*"

Her hands massaged mine with her fingers as she continued.

"Evie wasn't fully convinced so after Cami had gone to sleep, we went outside. It was summer. Hot even after midnight. I remember it being *so* hot. The grass was wet on our bare feet. Evie led me by the arm to the edge of woods and we sat down, trying to catch a cooling breeze. I remember being scared and wanting to go back inside. I stood up and Evie grabbed my arm. As I jerked away, there was a big snapping sound above us, like a gunshot…*CRAAACK!* and a big tree limb hit the ground like an explosion, branches flying in every direction in front of us. I was numb. None of the limb had so much as touched me, but I was in shock, you know, *frozen*. Meanwhile, Evie was *screaming*. I turned back to her and watched as the splintered branches and broken sticks covered her. I mean, they wrapped around her. They became *alive*. They became a person, a *man*. A grown-up man, bending her backwards by the throat with one hand. The other hand was raised above his head holding the biggest knife I've ever seen. The blade glowed, like it was electrified or something.

"'You're about to get yours,'" the man said. "I hollered at him and he stopped to look at me. Evie turned her head to me. Red tears spilled from dull grey eyes, running down her cheeks. I charged forward and launched myself into Evie and the phantom attacker. We hit the ground so hard, I was knocked out of breath. Underneath me, Evie was shuddering. She was holding onto me so hard, her nails dug into the skin under my shirt, leaving marks on my back for a couple of weeks."

Casey released my hands and clapped once.

"*Presto!* She was a believer!"

I felt like I was going to vomit.

"Yeah." I stood up, trying to shake off my growing nausea. "Good for her." I coughed twice to suppress dry heaving. "Good for you, too," I added.

Casey watched me go to the tarp. I turned my back on her.

"You think this is funny? *Normal?* You watched your parents' fake funeral. You saw your friend about to be gutted by some homicidal phantasm. You've put up with this since you were twelve years old?"

Casey came up behind me and put her hand on my shoulder.

"I don't think it's funny," she said.

Whirling around, I grabbed her arm. "It's *not* funny," I agreed.

"What're you doing?" she asked.

I pulled us through the split in the tarp and broke into a slow run pulling Casey behind. I stopped in the middle of the yard and raised my head to the sheltering black sky awash with blinking stars.

"I'm going to figure this out."

I watched a spark from a shooting star blaze across the night sky, filling me with confidence.

"Once and for all, for all of us."

Casey stepped in front of me and pointed into the trees.

"What is *that?*"

"Maybe it's a caterpillar with a spider face," I said, finding my newfound confidence flavored with sarcasm. "Maybe it's *our* funeral."

I started walking forward to the tree line with a strut in my step, only seeing what I wanted to see, only aware that I was growing angrier by the second. Behind me, Casey yanked me to a stop by the collar of my t-shirt.

"*THAT,*" she said, her outstretched arm over my shoulder, pointing her finger. "Don't you see it?"

I did.

Deep into the layers of trees moved a glowing figure. The size of a man, the figure moved forward and backward, left and right, growing brighter and dimming with each movement. The indistinct shape shimmered as it expanded and shrank. For an instant, I saw a square boxy head, bobbing up and down. The illuminated figure moved stiffly through the woods. As its light grew dim, threatening to vanish, I broke into a run, pulling Casey by her arm and shouting with an excited hiss, "*Let's get it!*"

The instant we crossed over the line into the trees, we became separated in the dark. Our footsteps crunched against the pine needles and dead leaves on the ground. "Follow my voice!" I yelled. "Keep going forward!"

"I'm here," Casey yelled back. "I'm right beside you!"

I ran through the trees, winding my way through saplings and hopping over dead limbs, faster and faster, keeping my eyes on the pinpoint of light from the retreating creature, my legs pumping up and down, arms rocking front and back like pistons at my sides. I was about to make short work of all this madness. I was running so fast, it felt like I was floating on air. I was going to solve this mystery, I thought as the dim light in the distance glowed brighter. I was going to put this—

—*nightmare*—

—*to rest*—

My feet left the ground.

—*once and for all*—

Both arms began to flail at nothing as my feet kicked against the air. My stomach rose into my throat.

I was in a freefall and heading to whatever lay below at a speed that took my breath away.

A cliff, I thought. In the dark, I'd run headlong off a cliff. *That's the end of me.* I braced for the final impact, squeezing my eyes shut as I splashed into a mixture of water and mud.

I'd tripped and fallen face-first into the pond.

What felt like a free-fall in a dream was nothing more than a stumble and spill. I was still alive. Raising my head from the water, I coughed out a mouthful of liquid and silt as I pulled myself out of the pond shallows.

"*There* you are," Casey called from somewhere on the bank. "You all right?"

"Soaked," I answered. When I turned, I saw Casey sitting on a log. Standing next to her was the Lighted Man. "*BESIDE YOU!*" I hollered a warning.

"He's real," Casey replied. "Get out of the water and come up here."

The Lighted Man raised his arm, holding his frozen wave above his head.

Now was the time I expected some hybrid alligator and octopus to burst out of the water and drag me down to the murky bottom of the pond. But neither an *Octogator* nor *Allopus* materialized.

I wiped my face and brushed back my hair, trying to clear off as much mud as I could. My right hand absently brushed over my left arm, fingers rolling over numb lumps on the skin from elbow to wrist, flabby pustules that my hand couldn't shake off.

I raised my arm in front of me and screamed.

It was mottled with black leeches. I slapped down as hard as I could to remove the bloodsuckers as I watched my fingers curl and turn white as my arm began to die from lack of blood. The leeches inflated like balloons on a canister of helium as they sucked away.

A brilliant, almost unbearably bright light fell over me.

"They're not real, son."

Everything around me was lit up clear as day, including my extended arm. The leeches were gone. Or rather, they had never been there in the first place.

The Lighted Man was in front of me, extending an open hand. In the other hand he held a portable spotlight, the type I'd seen hunters use. His fingers wagged an invitation for me to take the open hand, so I did. He led me to the log. I sat down next to Casey. She brushed my hair and slapped her hands over the back of my shirt, trying to clean me off best as she could.

The Lighted Man stood over us, hands behind his back as if it were just another night for him. I could see now that the man was dressed in a high-grade hazmat-type suit, the square helmet was lighted from the inside, giving his otherwise benevolent face an eerie yellow glow. When he spoke, his voice had an underlying tone of static from the built-in microphone, clicking each time he spoke and right after he stopped.

"Your light, it...it stopped them," I managed to get out with a stammer.

click. "Any direct light stops the Spirit Fog." *click.*

"The...what?"

"Spirit...fog?" Casey chimed in. "What the *fu*—"

click. "My turn. What're you kids doing out here? Are you runaways?" *click.*

Casey crossed her arms, locking them tight against her stomach. "We're eloping," she said with a defiant frown.

The Lighted Man rolled his eyes.

"My name is Julian Baker. This is Casey Woodruff. We were having a slumber party at my aunt and uncle's house."

click. "Your Uncle—*Vincent Baker?*" *click.*

"That's right, sir."

The Lighted Man put his hands behind his neck, uncoupling the square helmet and raising it from his head. He laid it on the ground at his feet.

Other lights inside the suit glowed from below, shining under his chin and over his face. He appeared to be the same age as Dad, maybe a few years older, give or take. His eyes were bright, his face sharp and lean, sculpted lines cut on either side of his nose, accentuating his cheeks and chin. How else to put it? He looked *smart*.

He pulled the right glove from the Hazmat suit, extending his bare hand to me. I reached out and we shook hands.

"Dr. Greer. Harlan Greer. *Very* pleased to meet you, Mr. Julian Baker." He let go of my hand.

With a slight turn to Casey, he offered her the same hand. "Ms. Woodruff?"

"Casey," she said, shaking his hand. "What are you doing up here?"

"Yeah. I'm wondering that myself," I said.

Dr. Harlan Greer retrieved his big square helmet off the ground. "Trying to solve a mystery." He put the helmet over his head, reaching behind to lock it in place.

click. "Same as you." *click.*

Chapter Nine

William and Lawrence

Dr. Harlan Greer led us through the woods to a waiting Subaru Forester. He stripped off the Haz-mat suit, cramming it into the back among the clutter of camping equipment and cases containing what I assumed were various types of equipment of some sort. He leaned back on the bumper under the open hatch, giving his t-shirt a few tugs to cool himself off. There was a headshot of Einstein on the shirt and quote which read *Imagination is more important than knowledge.*

I explained to him that this was only my second night here while Casey revealed that she'd been spending the night with her friends since she was thirteen.

"How old are you, Julian?"

"Almost seventeen."

He pointed to Casey.

"Almost sixteen."

Dr. Greer tilted his head at us. I could tell he was thinking about what to say next.

"*So...*" he began, drawing out the word to finish his thought. His eyes went to Casey. "You're telling me that in all that time, after over two years of experiencing...*this...*" he waved a hand in an arc over his head "...that your friends never told you a simple flashlight keeps the Spirit Fog from taking shape?"

Casey shook her head. "Maybe they didn't kno—"

"And Julian," he said turning to me. "Your dad didn't give you that basic information before your maiden voyage? Vincent didn't tell either one of you? *Very strange.*"

I finished Casey's explanation. "Maybe they didn't know."

Dr. Greer's palms slapped his knees. He stood up and closed the hatch. "I could be telling tales out-of-school here guys, I could be saying too much, but both of them know. At least about the whole light-thing."

"You know my dad and my uncle?"

"Another talk for another time," Dr. Greer said. "Pile in. I'll take you guys back to the house."

The Forester stopped at the edge of the tree line. Dr. Greer killed the lights. "Go straight about fifty feet and you'll come to a little bald spot. Take a sharp left as soon as you hit the opening into another stand of trees. Go straight again for another thirty yards and you'll come out into the back yard." He handed me a tiny maglite. "You got it?"

"I got it."

He had me repeat the directions. When I was finished, he passed me a small card. "Put this in your pocket. If I ever hear from you again, we'll finish the conversation." I took the card and we shook hands. "It was nice meeting you, Julian Baker."

"Yes, sir, Dr. Greer. Nice meeting you, too."

"Ms. Woodruff," he called to Casey in the back seat. "It's been a pleasure."

"Same here," Casey answered.

We watched as the Forester backed away from us and turned in the opposite direction, red taillights disappearing down the dark path. I switched on the mag light. Casey took hold of my arm as I followed the doctor's directions. Five minutes later, we could see the shadow of the second story of the house and then The Playhouse as we walked into the back yard. Casey let go of my arm, walking slightly ahead of me but making sure to remain in the rays of the maglite. We both went inside without a word between us. As she disappeared behind the partition, I stripped off my damp and muddy clothes, folding them into a tight ball. After retrieving a clean set of clothes from my bag, I stuffed the soiled wad at the bottom of the bag, zippered it shut and re-dressed. It was early Sunday morning.

I fell asleep thinking of Dad and wondering how the Vincennes gig went, knowing I would see him again in a handful of hours.

Rayven and I were halfway through watching *Army of Darkness* in his room when The Strays pulled into the driveway a few minutes after noon. I hadn't seen the twins or Casey at all after the sun had risen on Sunday and I hadn't said a word to Rayven about the night before. We'd returned a couple hours before dawn and it looked like no one was the wiser. I couldn't be sure, but I doubted if Casey had said anything to Evie or Cami. She wanted to come back, to spend future nights here with her friends. She knew the less she said, the better.

The prospect of going back down into Harris, back into the same old house doing the same old stuff with Dad filled me with a disappointment bordering on dread. Like Casey, I was not finished with the mystery. This was my reason for keeping silent, keeping my questions to myself. I was leaving, but I wanted desperately to come back soon. I wondered what Casey hoped she would find after all her times up here, even as I wondered the same about what discoveries awaited me.

Bruce Campbell fudged the words to send the Deadites back to oblivion when I heard the van honking its horn in the driveway as if signaling a cheap date.

Dad greeted me outside the van as I came out of the house. Uncle Vincent was close behind, walking in front of me to greet his brother. I stopped short, allowing them their moment.

Dad peered over Uncle Vincent's shoulder at me as they exchanged brief words. They hugged and Uncle Vincent headed back inside, stopping to hug me. "Come back anytime, Julian. You're always welcome," he said, going inside the house before I could respond. Dad greeted me with tired eyes and a handshake. "Good weekend?"

"Yeah, we did some fishing, caught a few nice ones."

I noticed Dad was driving and the passenger seat was empty. Climbing in and taking shotgun beside him, I saw Finny, Scott, and Jack taking up the rear. All but Scott was asleep and he was probably only awake because he had Finny's head on one shoulder, Jack's on the other. Wedged between the two, Scott could only shrug his eyebrows at me, looking first at Finny, then to Jack. *"Lightweights,"* he said. "Whaddaya gonna do?"

"Try not to let 'em smother you," Dad offered as he drove away from the house.

"How was the show?"

"Two good ones," answered Dad.

"Full house both nights," Scott added.

I looked back at him. "Oh, man, Scott. Finny's drooling on your shirt."

Scott lurched forward and cursed. Still sleeping, Finny and Jack folded into each other behind Scott. Their heads knocked together and they came awake with a start, groggily blaming each other as Scott leaned forward between me and Dad.

"How was your weekend, *Big J?*" he asked.

"Okay," I said, barely hearing Scott's voice. I was thinking about Casey, what she was doing right now, realizing I'd never told her goodbye. I wondered if she was thinking the same thing. The thoughts made me sad, but I embraced the emotion, nevertheless. It was a deep sadness, yet somehow comforting.

———

Dad dropped me off at our house first before taking the rest of The Strays home. I knew he would be gone for at least three hours; not only would he have to take Scott and Jack home, but they would also all have to unload the gear at Finny's house, where they rehearsed. Shagged as they all were from the weekend, I didn't expect to see Dad again until late evening.

I threw my bag on the floor of my bedroom and walked the two blocks to Casey's convenience store and gas station, getting four chicken legs and an order of fries from the short-order counter. Back home, I devoured the feast cross-legged on the floor before unpacking my bag.

I'd all but forgotten about the pond-soaked clothes until my hand squished into the soggy bundle at the bottom of the bag. I pulled them out with a sour grimace. Still wet, the rolled bundle made a moist slap against the floor. "Yuck," I said aloud. No matter. Short work to throw the bundle in the washing machine. Unfolding the wad of clothes, I separated socks from underwear, t-shirt from jeans. Checking the pockets of the jeans, my fingers connected with something in a back pocket. A damp business card.

Harlan Greer, Ph.D.
Neuroscientist
Department of Clinical Psychology
Indiana State University, Office 212
812-240-5489

I stuck the card to the small cork bulletin board above my desk with a black pushpin.

Should I call him or not? Would he even remember me, I thought, even though it had been only a few hours before that I'd met Dr. Harlan Greer, Ph.D., Neuroscientist, no less.

Of course, he'd remember me. I looked over at the phone on my nightstand, building my courage.

It was Sunday afternoon. I had school the next day. Then I'd be able to catch up with Rayven and especially Casey.

Emptying my bag into the wash, I thought about what I would say. Would there even be a chance to talk about what we saw? Maybe at lunch.

After taking a shower, I was hungry again but by that time it was ten 'o clock at night. Still no sign of Dad.

I turned on the porch light and left the light above the kitchen sink burning before slipping into bed, pulling the sheet and blanket under my chin and falling into a deep sleep.

The next day, to my surprise, Casey treated me like a stranger. Seeing her coming out of the gym, I hollered her name as I passed by on the way to my Biology II class. Her eyes flashed in my direction for a second before she continued in the opposite direction without a word. I knew she'd seen me.

"She ghosted me big time," I told Rayven as we sat at lunch, careful to not let Roger Gallo and Bill Purcell hear my concern as they ate their tepid cheeseburgers across the long table.

Rayven, on the other hand, wasn't so subtle. He might as well have had a megaphone. "I thought you *hated* Creepy Casey!"

Roger Gallo threw a packet of ketchup across the table, barely missing my head. It sailed over my head and landed on the floor. "Cradle Robber!" he yelled.

"She's a sophomore. We're seniors." I stared him down, daring him to say something else. Bill Purcell was giggling into his tray at Gallo's joke.

Rayven came halfway off his seat and leaned toward them.

"Both of you better shut the fuck up." He hooked their trays with his index fingers and pulled them both to him. "Besides, you're done. Lunch is over."

Gallo stood up and apologized. He'd weighed the odds with Rayven many times before and knew that, indeed, lunch was over. "I didn't mean nothing, Julian," he said, apologizing again.

Purcell, always slow to catch on with such social interactions, kept his seat, bewildered. "Can I get my milk?"

Gallo pulled him from his seat. "C'mon, get a drink at the fountain in the hallway," he said, leading him out like a stubborn horse.

"I *like* her, man. I mean, I *really* like her." Finding the right words was an almost impossible struggle as I tried to explain.

"Nothing wrong with that."

"We saw the same, you know...*things* over the weekend. After everyone was asleep." The lunch period was almost over. I wasn't ready to tell him the details of the shared adventure. Anyway, there wasn't enough time.

"Nothing wrong with that, either." Rayven regarded the trays he'd confiscated from Gallo and Purcell. "Want some more fries?"

Instead of going home after school, the idea of stopping at the library came to me. The library should have records on the Black Diamond Mine, Crumpton Hill, or both. It was a Monday and Mondays meant little to no homework and nothing else to do outside of school. I'd been ghosted by Casey, confronted with Rayven's tight-lipped nonchalance over the whole situation, and generally had had a piss-poor day. There was nothing to lose by spending a few minutes surrounded by aisles of books and silence. It was a ten-minute walk from McKinley High and ten more minutes and six blocks to my house from there, so time wasn't a factor either way. I'd been walking the same route home since my sophomore year. It was one of the perks of living in Harris, a perk I assumed stretched to probably every small town across the country.

Stopping at the bottom of the long cement steps leading up to the library entrance, I sat down on the first step and dug into the bottom of my backpack for my phone, hoping it still held a charge. The battery was at 15%. More than enough for my purpose.

I texted *Stopped at library after school, home soon* and Dad's reply was familiar and instant: *10-4*. I dropped the phone into my backpack and headed up the steps.

Although I practically lived on my computer playing games in my free time, I wasn't much for e-mail or social media. In Harris, the technology was hit-or-miss. Atop Crumpton Hill, it was non-existent. Rayven and his sisters didn't even own cell phones. A few people at McKinley swore by their cellphones; *lived* by social media, but they were the exception, a clutch of students blessed by the circumstances of their parents all the while confusing their birthright for entitlement, rather than luck. I couldn't tell you their names, nobody we knew hung around with them. Like us, they were in their own manufactured worlds. But they were a minority. Another perk of living in Harris. Most of us still relied on daily face-to-face interactions. Most of us still retained a certain skill of social interaction, as awkward and frightening as it often was. But we were learning about the world, whether we knew it or not. We were learning that anger was not a sustainable feeling between people. We were learning courage in circumstances where courage was called for, rather than the cowardice of anonymity in *every* circumstance. We didn't have any *likes.* But we liked a lot of others who liked us in return. Certainly, growing up in Harris was not a badge of worldliness. Moreover, it lacked any culture beyond a local understanding of what it meant to be sophisticated.

I'll have to find those things out for myself, in my own way, I thought as the library doors closed lazily behind me. I was immersed between the odor of aging paper and the confluence of all manner of volumes and knowledge. Impressive even for Harris, Indiana.

"I'm looking for everything you have on the town. It's for an essay in my Senior English Class."

The Librarian tilted her head, eyes narrowing. "*Everything, huh?* That's a pretty broad subject for a high school paper. Can you narrow that down?"

She wasn't what I'd expected after my first visit to the small yet stately town library in almost ten years. My remembered stereotype of an elderly woman with a tedious manner was my own bias, thus my own mistake. This woman had a vibrant demeanor, wearing a cotton pastel short-sleeve blouse accentuating high-breasts with a hint of cleavage over the low-cut collar. One nostril was pierced with a single silver ring. She was no one I knew from school, nobody's older sister. She had to be from ISU in Terre Haute. A college student.

"*Hello?*" she said impatiently, shocking me out of my silent analysis. "You'll have to narrow down your subject, young man."

That threw me *way* off, the young man thing. I blurted out: "Mines. The Black Diamond Mine. The history of the mine."

"Oh." She relaxed in her chair as if relieved I hadn't asked her personally how to split the atom. "That's an easy one," she said. "One book on that very subject." Leaving the desk, she left me standing there as she weaved her way through the aisles before returning with a thin book. She asked for my library card. "Can I look at it here?"

She handed me the book and motioned to three lines of empty tables in the center of the room. "Take your pick."

I thanked her and sat down on a chair in the middle of the center table, placing the book on the tabletop between my hands.

AMERICAN ENTREPRENEURS:
THE SELF-MADE JOURNEY OF WILLIAM CHESTERTON

For the next two hours my frustration grew with each page I read. Born in upstate New York into a relatively nondescript life, the only son of a tailor and housewife, Lawrence Muldoon grew into a mundane adulthood. A bank teller from his late teens into his mid-twenties, there was no indication his future held anything other than the same life his father had achieved. Those who knew him related that he was unmotivated and not a particularly great thinker, much less a visionary. By the time I came to the part about him heading west to follow in the footsteps of his peers in the hope of seeking his fortune, my eyelids became anchors I struggled to raise with each sentence.

American Entrepreneur? You've got to be shitting me.

About to close the book in frustration, I caught a glimpse of the words ...*met William Chesterton*...and continued to read.

At thirty years-old, William Blankenship Chesterton was already an established Pennsylvania coal-baron. At the turn of the century, as immigrants poured into New York from Ireland and Italy, young Chesterton was on his way to becoming a millionaire when he met Lawrence Muldoon in a West Virginia train depot.

Muldoon was making his way out to Colorado when he became stranded in Bluefield, West Virginia where it so happened that William Chesterton was finalizing his Welch Mine operation. The two met in a company tavern next to the railroad tracks in Bluefield late on the third evening of Muldoon's ongoing dilemma of begging nickels from the locals. They took up conversation quite by, what Lawrence would call years later, a "happy accident."

William characterized it thusly: *After drinking long into the night, we spent the next day commiserating in a most animated fashion in the back room behind the same tavern where we began, called Boatsy's. I owned the establishment, having bought it a week before meeting Larry in the hope of fashioning it into a place where the Welch miners would feel at home after their workday. The more we talked, the more I realized he had qualities I simply didn't possess. I've always been a bottom-line businessman. Larry, on the other hand, was a talker. He was a politician. It became clear to me that if we combined our unique skills, we could achieve more financial success and control over the mining market as any dozen competing partnerships.*

As to who formed the title of their corporation neither could say, but both would claim the credit.

Lawrence was passed out when I came up with the name of our partnership.

Bill was fast asleep across the single rope-bed cot in the room when I came up with our corporate name.

Chesterton-Muldoon Enterprises.

Ches-ter-ton...Mol-dern...

I slapped the book away from me. It stopped on the far side of the table, still open and accusing. I half-expected the book to lurch back into my hands.

Frollo-Ches-Ter-Ton-Moldern

Leaving the book where it lay, I offered a weak *thank you* to the pretty librarian as I hurried out the door. I had to get home. The business card on my bulletin board glowed in my head, calling me with a frenzied urgency. It was time to make a phone call.

Chapter Ten

A Conversation

Liars are contemptible. Those who lie in order to cheat and steal and tout non-existent accomplishments are beyond reproach. To me, a lie and arrogance are equal offenses and oftentimes go hand-in-hand.

This is much different than the *Fake It Until You Make It* philosophy. In fact, I would argue that this mindset is better paraphrased by *Keep Your Mouth Shut as You Learn*. Arrogance has no place in the mind of the apprentice.

Similarly, telling a lie does not make one a capital *"L" liar*. But then again, I'm only rationalizing the lie I told Dad to borrow the Jeep so I could drive the fifteen miles to Terre Haute to meet Dr. Harlan Greer in his office at Indiana State University.

"I'm meeting with a counselor to get some information on attending college next year," I told him. There was no arguing with the lie. Dad tossed me the keys and told me to drive safely without so much as blinking. The nature of the lie was harmless, I thought. I *was* going to ISU to meet with a representative of the University. And who knows? Perhaps I would attend ISU after graduating in the spring.

After texting on Monday, *I want to talk about stuff* to the number on his card, Dr. Greer took two days to text back *Saturday at noon. In my office.* That was on Thursday.

Friday night saw me lying to Dad and securing the keys to the Jeep.

There's not much difference between a high school campus and a college campus. At first glance, their uninviting buildings are dull and foreboding from the outside.

Passing through the entrance to a high school is intimidating, to say the least. Once inside, the building is confusing at best.

A college campus is the same, except you must figure out which foreboding building from a half-dozen other buildings to choose from providing you're on the right sidewalk leading to the building you need.

Once inside a high school, you stroll under bright lights everywhere you go. The atmosphere is antiseptic and reeks of stale, recirculated air.

Every time you open the door and go inside of any college building, a damp and musty odor is so prevalent as to make one stop under dim light and take in a deep breath. Some students refer to this phenomenon light-heartedly as the smell of knowledge, while others simply ignore it.

As I made my way down the hallway of the Faculty Building looking for Office 212, my nostrils smelled only moldy decay. I advanced haltingly under cheap lighting that flickered like wax-and-wick candelabra flame illuminating my path. The atmosphere was charged with mystery and seemed so much larger than my small world or anything I could ever hope to become. I was no match for these long-standing Gothic halls filled with haunted shadows. How could I ever be worthy of such stately mansions of higher learning?

Mr. Baker! Down here!

The voice echoed over the hallway from what seemed like miles away. Startled, I lurched to a halt. Dr. Greer's head was poking out from an open doorway on the right. He motioned me to him and I broke into an uneasy trot.

Compared to the dim and claustrophobic hallway, inside his office was like something from *Doctor Who*; an expanse of tiled floor and high ceilings, ten-foot bookshelves on every side of the room. In the center, a mammoth desk made of dark wood over which piles of papers and magazines and file folders were stacked high enough to obscure a well-worn tall-backed brown leather chair beyond. Dr. Harlan Greer, Ph.D., deep inside his personal TARDIS.

He closed the door behind us as I entered, pulling a rickety office chair up to the front of his desk meant for me. Obediently, I sat down as Dr. Greer took up his seat on the other side of the desk. He settled into the high-backed chair, clasping his hands in his lap.

"It's nice to see you again," he said like he didn't mean it. "What can I do for you?"

"In the woods, you said I could call, that we could talk." Unable to keep eye contact, my eyes flitted from his chin to the desktop to my shoes.

"You want to know how I know your dad and uncle."

I fidgeted, trying to shrink. "Sure. That was a surprise, but there are other things. I don't know where to start."

Dr. Greer's chair creaked as it came forward to the edge of the desk. He laid his palms flat on the top of the dark wood.

"Something else happened to you. Since we met."

He wasn't exactly right, but I nodded. I told him about the Play-Doh head and my visit to the library where I was introduced to Chesterton-Muldoon Enterprises. When I finished, my eyes finally met his. I immediately wanted to look away but forced myself to keep both eye contact and silence.

The man's eyes were afire under his furrowed brow. Whether he was shocked, surprised, angry, or something else, I didn't know. Finally, I saw his brow relax, the fire in his eyes going from an intense blaze to a reflective glow.

"*Frollo Chesterton Moldern,*" he said softly, thinking through each word as he spoke it. "Are you sure that's right? That's what you heard?"

"Yes, sir," I said with a vigorous nod.

He cleared his throat. "Well."

111

I waited for him to finish but the word hung between us for an interminable amount of time. Just as I thought I would jump out of my skin, Dr. Greer leaned back into his chair once more.

"*Moldern* is obviously Muldoon. *Frollo...*" He repeated the word several times before paraphrasing what I'd heard.

"Frollo Chesterton Muldoon. And you're positive you heard *Frollo?*"

I nodded.

"Hmmm," he said, fingers tracing the line of his goatee.

"So, Chesterton-Muldoon Enterprises owned the Black Diamond Coal Mine, started the operation, in fact. You won't hear this from any amateur historians in the area, but it was doomed from the start, a real *cut-corners* operation. Shoddy and unsafe from the first day. It was a miracle the mine produced and operated for as long as it did. There was the occasional accident common to every mining operation, but the Black Diamond Mine was living on borrowed time from day one. The only people who knew it at the time were Chesterton and his investors. Of course, all the corruption is common knowledge now, it's just not part of the lexicon of local history."

"The Little Italy Festival."

Dr. Greer tilted his head. "I don't follow."

"The Little Italy Festival," I repeated, exclaiming, "It's so obvious! The whole town of Harris knows it's all a rotten lie!"

"Now, wait...wait a minute, Julian."

Dr. Greer stood up. He loosened his tie and unbuttoned his collar.

"The '*whole town*' of Harris, as you put it, doesn't know any such thing, whether they're aware of the facts or not. The Little Italy Festival isn't a celebration of the coal mine, it's a celebration of the town's founders. The Black Diamond Mine gave a lot of those early families a good living and the opportunity the town needed to survive, corrupt management aside. What happened wasn't right and never needed to happen, but for the greed and slimy opportunism of Bill Chesterton, that's a fact. Reality is a strange thing, my young friend. Reality is fluid and has many tributaries. It doesn't run in a tidy razor-sharp line. Thirty-five men died in the explosion and no one else ever went into

112

those shafts again. The mine was closed, the dead were mourned. Like the coal hauled out of there prior to the disaster, the trove of benefits for the town realized from that same hole couldn't be denied, either. Do you understand? The Little Italy Festival celebrates the Black Diamond Mine only insofar as the *good* things it produced. You know that. The Coal Town Museum, the Harris train depot hosts during the festival, doesn't try to cover-up the explosion but doesn't celebrate it either. Gino understood that better than anyone. The old man proudly hosted the museum every year for decades before he died. He loved volunteering for that, looked forward to it as the only survivor of the explosion."

"*Checko*," I whispered.

"That's right," Dr. Greer continued. "Did you know he came over here from Italy after his parents were murdered by the ruling syndicate in his hometown? He had to leave because they were looking for him, too, to end the family line as was custom over there at that time. He came over with an older boy, who watched over him while they were on the ship. His family had been killed in similar fashion, halfway across Italy from where Gino—*Checko*—lived."

"I knew Checko. He was my friend."

As Dr. Greer paced back and forth on the other side of his desk, going from one end of the office to the other, he shrugged the palm of one hand at me.

"Sorry, I didn't know. I tend to go on and on. He told you all this."

"No," I said. "All he ever told me about was being rescued from the mine. I never knew his real name was Gino or any of that other stuff."

Dr. Greer stopped pacing. "He never told you about Michael?"

"I don't know any Michael."

Closing his eyes, Dr. Greer snapped his fingers in one ear as he went *umm umm umm*—at last breaking into a smile and exclaiming *"That's it!"* as if to congratulate his brain.

"Mutt!" he yelled. "That was his nickname. He was in the mine with Checko that day. He was the older kid who came over from Italy with Checko. *Michael Generro*."

113

I was still reeling from what I'd just heard; so many revelations shattering my notions of things I'd previously assumed I knew backwards and forwards. My head felt like an ever-expanding balloon straining to make space for more air to the bursting point. My first instinct was to thank Dr. Greer and get the hell out of there as fast as possible and forget everything I knew and was finding out. It's too much, I thought, I can't take it. I felt a fast-rising hysteria threaten to overtake me, so I took a deep breath and embraced the electrical chills firing through my body. Faster than I can describe, my fear turned to stubbornness and the stubbornness turned to courage. My curiosity was recharged once more, ready for anything. Or so I thought.

"...you know the rest, right?" Dr. Greer continued. "Almost immediately after the explosion, William Chesterton closed the Black Diamond Mine, packed up kit-and-kaboodle, and left Indiana."

"I didn't get that far in the book at the library," I confessed.

Dr. Greer nodded understanding. "Once you saw the connection to your Play-Doh head friend—"

"Yeah, I was out of there."

"Can't blame you. Completely normal reaction." He leaned over me, emphasizing the point. "*Completely* normal reaction." He resumed pacing, head bowed in concentration. "Where was I—*yeah*. After Chesterton left Indiana, he tried his hand at establishing some mines out in western Colorado, but news of thirty-five dead miners travels fast and travels far. It became apparent that ol' Bill's mining pursuits were over. He spent the rest of his life running a fairly successful mercantile store...a hardware store...in Ogden, Utah."

I considered that for a moment before remembering something else.

"What about Lawrence Muldoon? Where did he end up?"

Dr. Greer belly laughed. "He paid off the sins of his partner, didn't he? Sorry to laugh, but you must admit the irony kinda overrides that whole tragedy."

Bewildered, I shook my head. "You lost me."

Dr. Greer blushed. His mouth dropped open without forming words as he stared at me. The reaction flew in the face of my image of him to this point. I thought he might be having a sudden heart attack. I started to stand up. *"Dr. Greer?"*

"It was a bad joke," he said. "I thought you knew."

I pressed back into my seat, aware of my hands clutching the arms of the chair. I was at the top of the rollercoaster tracks, holding on for dear life an instant before the inevitable plunge. My body language was so pronounced, so obvious to Dr. Greer, I didn't have to say a word.

"Larry Muldoon died in the mine that day."

I closed my eyes to brace myself as my stomach rose into my chest. The blood from my feet rushed to my head. I was overtaken with an intense dizziness and sensation of falling from a great distance. The feeling lasted only a second or two and was gone.

"No one can say for sure at what point Muldoon knew of the safety issues, the cost-cutting measures, and the resulting dangerous conditions because of his partner's all-consuming greed. Larry Muldoon was a lot of things; a glad hander, a politician…a *bullshit peddler*, but he wasn't heartless. He was Bill Chesterton's business partner, but he had what Chesterton lacked. He had compassion. On the day of the explosion, Muldoon had decided he'd had enough of the deception. He was going to close the mine come hell or high-water. Why he didn't call the miners back to the surface by radio is a mystery for the ages. He got into the elevator and was headed down to warn everyone when the explosion happened."

"Checko told me about Mutt. About how he stayed with Mutt because Mutt's arm was trapped in the shaft when the elevator derailed from the explosion. He never mentioned anyone else. He never said there was anyone inside the elevator."

"He wouldn't have known, Julian." Dr. Greer sighed. "I'm not sure he ever found out after the fact. When that elevator hit the bottom of the shaft where Gino and Michael were, Lawrence Muldoon must have been reduced to something resembling a wet canvas sack. He would have been unrecognizable as a person. You have two friends in the middle of a life-or-death situation with slim chances of survival for either one. Plus, it's almost pitch black. The last thing you're going to worry about, if you even notice it all, is a pile of mush inside an elevator you can't see into anyway."

It made sense. Lawrence Muldoon was one of the first *whistleblowers*. To this day, it's a dangerous position to take. Back then, the potential repercussions must have been unfathomable, the risks beyond limit. It made perfect sense.

"Checko told me the story about what happened to him fifty years or more after the fact. Are you saying in all that time, he never learned about Muldoon, about what he was trying to do?"

"That's what I'm saying, son. Lawrence Muldoon the person is all but erased from written record."

"So, thirty-six people died that day, not thirty-five."

"No, Julian. Thirty-five *miners* died that day. You have to understand that. Take any tragedy, whether it be an explosion or a tornado or a hurricane, fire, what have you. Where a business is concerned, you always hear the fatalities referred to as *workers* or *employees*. Right or wrong, it's the way of things."

"Does anyone know about how Muldoon died? Has he ever gotten his due for being such a hero for what he did?"

Dr. Greer motioned to himself with both hands.

"Stupid question," I admitted. "But how did you find this out? How are you the only one who knows about this?"

"*Ah, there's the rub.*" He came up to me and patted my shoulders. "I never said I was the only one who knew about how Muldoon died. In fact, I imagine tens of thousands of people know about Muldoon's fate in that elevator. Oh, there's been no books written about it. Whenever his name is mentioned beyond the Black Diamond Mine, the biographical notes invariably repeat phrases like *whereabouts unknown* or give a death-date with a qualifying caveat such *est.* or a range of three years. There are no books about the Black Diamond Coal Mine, no comprehensive history of the operation. Likewise, there are no books about Lawrence Muldoon. You found the single book on William Chesterton ever written. An anemic tome about a minor player in what amounts to almost ancient history."

"So much hidden truth," I breathed in a thin sigh.

"Impossible to discover it all," Dr. Greer finished. "But isn't just knowing *that* pretty damn mind-blowing?"

I nodded.

"And that's just here, at this insignificant point in time we occupy. Imagine the larger implications."

I nodded again.

Dr. Greer slapped his knees, same as he'd done that first night leaning against the mud-caked Forester. This time, I knew what the action indicated: he was about to end our meeting.

"Mr. Baker, I've enjoyed our time—"

"How do you know my dad and my uncle?"

Dr. Greer glanced at his wristwatch. "It's 2:30 in the afternoon. We've been talking for over two hours."

"It's Saturday. I've nothing to do and all the time in world," I said boldly, squaring my shoulders and sitting up straight to emphasize the point.

Dr. Greer's body deflated. He slumped back against the front of his desk.

"It *is* Saturday, that's true. I've got no classes today." He rubbed his chin as he gazed at the ceiling. "I've got no date to meet for dinner and a movie. No pets at my little campus bungalow to feed. I didn't leave the stove on, or the water running..." he finished with a chuckle, flashed me the peace-sign and hitched himself up to a sitting position on the desktop.

"How do I know your uncle and dad, that was the question, right? Of course, it was. You want a bottle of water, some coffee...?"

My smile was so broad, I thought my lips would split apart. "I'm good, sir."

He hopped off the desk. "Not me. Excuse me for a second."

Disappearing into what I thought was a bathroom, Dr. Greer reappeared carrying two bottles of water. He handed one bottle to me before taking up his seat on the desktop. Opening his bottle, he took a long drink. "Much better," he declared. "I needed that." He pointed to the bottle in my hand. "Just in case."

I raised the bottle in a grateful salute. I'd liked Dr. Greer from the first time we met in the woods. *He's a good guy*, I remember thinking. But right now, sitting here with the man in his office, I felt a familiar kinship and trust, a feeling I'd only ever felt between me and Dad. A song lyric rolled across my mind, bringing both comfort and clarity.

This is the day of the expanding Man.

Indeed. I was embracing the bombardment of knowledge. I welcomed learning what I had been blind to before. The fear was fading fast, leaving only a burning determination to solve a greater mystery.

"I met Vincent before your dad, John. You were just a baby then. It was a few months after Vincent bought the house up there." Dr. Greer stopped and closed his eyes for the briefest of moments, like a long blink. "That was so many years ago." He stopped again, memories flooding his senses. His voice was faint. "*Wow.* I was so young back then. How is it that I became so old, here today? The simple passage of time. Such an easily understood part of the human condition. It strikes me as strange just the same."

I nodded. Dr. Greer had put words to what I'd been feeling for the last year of my own life.

He clapped his hands and I jumped at the sound.

"Anyway, I tried to buy the house from Vincent. I was persistent until he sent someone to visit me who said...*what did he say*...yeah, that's right: *'Fuck off and leave us alone or I'll beat you until you piss blood for a week.'* That was my introduction to your father."

I gasped. "Dad said that to you?"

Dr. Greer noted my shocked expression and laughed.

"Sure. He was just protecting his brother's interests."

"What did you do?"

"I didn't do anything. I got the message loud and clear. Pissing blood implies a pretty serious injury, something I was neither excited about, nor had the time to spare for recovery from such an injury."

"So, you knew. You knew before anyone else."

"*Knew...?*"

"About what comes out at night."

Hopping off the desktop, Dr. Greer kneeled in front of me and took my hands in his.

"Those things that everyone sees, Julian, they just don't come out at night. They're always there. I've been coming to Crumpton Hill for over fifteen years to study the phenomenon. Sometimes I trespass on Vincent's property, but mostly I focus on the area around the mine, beyond what your uncle owns. The mine is the key to all of it, you see? I've been down inside that hole, explored all its tunnels, I've seen the elevator shaft."

Dr. Greer let go of my hands and stood up.

"I know why all of this happening. At least I think I do. What I'm trying to say is that I know where the things rising from the mine to walk the ground above come from. After so many years, I think I know how to stop it. I think I've found the pocket."

"*The pocket?*" I asked.

"The source," Dr. Greer answered. "Where all this is coming from. It's nothing but expanding energy, trapped for decades with nowhere to go. Slivers of it have been venting from the ground through ant colonies, mole burrows, and snake holes for a generation…that's what everyone has been seeing."

"I don't understand."

"Welcome to the club," Dr. Greer said with a sardonic smile. "There's a ground-level path down into the mine to the spot I've been studying for a long time. Beyond the elevator, to a deadfall of timbers and rocks. Where the thirty-five men were trapped. I've been digging through that mess to reach their location for years. I'm close now. I'm sure that's where the source will be. I'd bet my life on it." He cleared his throat and clapped his hands again before turning away from me.

"That's it, Mr. Julian Baker. That's the story according to me. I've told you everything I can. How I know your uncle and father, how I know about the phantoms you and your friends have seen and what I think is causing it all. The only thing I don't know is how to stop it, but I have a pretty good idea I want to try."

"You want to blow up Crumpton Hill."

"No," said Dr. Greer. "I think that ballooning energy, whatever it is, is sending a sort of distress signal. I want to make contact with it, help it if I can."

He made it sound like a living, intelligent thing with a conscious purpose. Fantastic as it was, I couldn't disagree.

"For the past few months, I've restricted my studies to what happens above the mine, gathering data. Over and over, the results have come out the same. I have to go down into the mine again. This time, I have to finish the dig I began when you were in elementary school and my hair was brown instead of silver. I'm going down tomorrow morning. Wanna come with me?"

Chapter Eleven

Descent

The entrance to the Black Diamond Mine, as Dr. Greer told me the day before, was at ground level. Originally a venting hole on the side of Crumpton Hill to be used as an alternate route to transport coal in single manually powered rail cars, it had been largely forgotten after proving impractical.

The surrounding area had been clear-cut for easy access. A well-maintained handcar sat a few feet inside the opening, secured by a heavy steel cable. The other end of the cable was attached to a formidable free-standing winch outside the entrance. Harlan Greer wasn't kidding. By the sight before me, it was clear he'd spent years on this project. A week ago, it was his personal mission to solve this mystery, one man's obsession. As I walked beside him to the jagged opening, I wondered if he realized he was walking next to someone who finally shared what had been his long and solitary pursuit. In for a penny, in for a pound, Dr. Greer had found himself a partner at last.

Before going in, he explained the logistics of our impending journey along with the strategy of reaching our goal.

"We can save a lot of time using the handcar rather than walking the rails." He pointed to the winch. "Once at the bottom, there's no way we can power the handcar ourselves to get back up here. There's a wireless winch control we'll use to pull the car back up. If the winch fails, we can walk the tracks back up. It's a gradual grade, ultimately a

200-foot climb, give or take a dozen feet or so. Or we can each lug a pick and shovel over our shoulders and walk down from here, but then we have to walk back up again."

Barely listening to him, my mind was on the probability of seeing phantoms ghastlier than a Play-Doh head and action figures come to life. "What about the white suits?"

Dr. Greer looked up into the morning sky. "It's daylight," he said, as if the reason should have been obvious to me. "We don't need 'em. We'll wear mining helmets with wheat lights and each carry a heavy-duty flashlight."

"Okay," I nodded.

"I suggest we take the handcar to the bottom. It gets a little hairy going down, there's some drops and jerks, but the cable keeps us steady. We have to walk about a couple-thousand yards once we're down there to get to the dig."

I nodded again, more unsure and nervous than before. "Okay. I'm ready."

Dr. Greer slapped me on the back. "It's a piece of cake, trust me."

I started to sweat. "Okay," I repeated a third time.

We stepped onto the handcar on opposite sides. Dr. Greer turned on his wheat light and I did the same. He grabbed the walking arm in both hands. "Up and down," he explained. "Like a seesaw." I grabbed onto the handles.

Without warning, the handcar lurched backward as Dr. Greer pulled the walking arm upward. "Now you," he said quickly. I pulled up as he pushed down. The car gained momentum as we settled into a rhythm. "Keep your eyes on me," Dr. Greer advised. "It'll start feeling a little weird, but everything's fine."

He wasn't wrong. Within a minute or two, I felt like I was perpetually falling backward in slow-motion as the track descended away from the daylight. "Up and down, that's right," he encouraged. "Slow and steady." All I could see was the light from my helmet, flashing up and down. The strobing glare revealed snapshots of the ceiling, my hands on the walking arm, and Dr. Greer's determined face as I pumped the handle in a death-grip. The feeling of falling backward grew more intense; I lost all sense of up and down, no matter how much I blinked to right myself. I took deep breaths, telling myself that Dr. Greer was experiencing the same sensation in reverse. That is, he must have felt as though he was falling *forward*.

The air became thin and dusty, suddenly much cooler.

"Ease up," Dr. Greer said, letting go of the walking arm as the handcar slowed. He reached down beside him to a long lever, giving it a gentle pull. The wheels of the handcar squeaked against the rails, coming to a stop.

Navigating the tunnels was no easy task. There were multiple paths and switchbacks in channels so narrow we had to walk single file, sometimes on our knees. Each of us carried a pickaxe and shovel, complicating the journey. My hands were already black with coal dust, before doing any actual work. I gasped for breath in the heavy atmosphere. What the hell was I doing down here?

I thought of coal miners, of the type of people they must have been and must be to this day making a living gladly visiting Hell every day of their workweek.

Stoic and courageous, these were people whose sense of responsibility to their families had to be on a supernatural scale. Beyond comic book superheroes, police officers and firefighters, coal miners were in a class by themselves.

We gathered up our shovels and pickaxes. Dr. Greer grinned at me. "Nicely done," he said. "Getting down here can be a little scary."

I exhaled. "A *little* scary."

He laughed. "The rest is easy. Only about a mile walk from here. Follow me."

"*A mile?* You said a couple thousand yards."

"Right," Dr. Greer said. He went forward into another tunnel. "Couple thousand yards *is* a mile."

He was right. I scrambled to follow him, embarrassed at my obvious ignorance.

Although the walk was easy, I was glad to follow behind Dr. Greer. Within fifteen minutes, we encountered two intersections of tunnels. I would have been lost on my own had it not been for his easy stride into the correct opening without so much as a single hesitant step. We came out into a large opening. Dr. Greer stopped, pointing to his left.

There it was. The ruined elevator.

I stepped up beside him, the beam of my wheat light merging with his, illuminating the corroded steel frame of the crooked cage protruding from its shaft.

"Once they pulled it up, once Gino Muciarelli was free, they let it fall again. I imagine between all that action, Muldoon's body had been scattered over the ground, the walls of the shaft, the elevator floor. *Vaporized.*"

Venturing closer to the elevator, I focused on the right side where Mutt Generro's arm had been trapped. All I could see was mottled rusty steel. Pointing my wheat light into the elevator, I hoped to see shreds of cloth from Lawrence Muldoon's clothes. All there was inside was a crushed and rusted bucket.

I was standing in the same spot as Checko seconds before the explosion. I was standing inside the story he'd told me; I was right there and could almost feel what he must have been feeling—a sense of panic, of dread. I reached out and touched the elevator, running my fingers lightly over the crusted surface.

A voice said, "He's gone."

I whispered, "I know," to Dr. Greer, turning to my left where he stood. My wheat light found only craggy black walls and rotting timbers where he had stood inches from me a second before.

From behind me came the same voice. "That's right. He's gone, my young friend."

Whirling around I came face to face with Checko. He was as I remembered, a stooped old man wearing a greasy white apron. His gentle face greeted me, ghostly in the shadow-filled light.

"He died in my arms. In this way, he was the first to escape." Checko reached out to me with an open hand.

Against my better judgment, my hand came forward and met his. Instead of my fingers passing through a discorporate image, I felt the cold, gelatinous touch of the dead old man. Beyond us, Dr. Greer was studying the walls, oblivious to what was happening.

124

"I thought I escaped, too. For all those years afterwards." Letting go of my hand, Checko turned a circle as he looked around. At the sight of Dr. Greer, he paused and pointed silently at him before completing his circle back to face me.

"But lately I've found myself here. Can you tell me why?"

I stared dumbfounded without words as Checko pleaded.

"Can you help me?"

"I don't think I can." I heard myself say. "No, I don't think so." I took a step forward to the flickering phantom of my dead friend. "I need to help the people left behind. Do you understand? I need to stop what's happening to my family and friends. That's why I'm here."

Checko bowed his head and nodded. "I think I understand."

"You're not trapped here. Not like you think. Mutt, either. He's gone. You lived a long life above this hole for years. Long after what happened to you down here."

"Yes. I can hear Mutt, but he's not here."

"That's right. He's not here because you were with him when he passed. He left this place long ago." How I was coming up with this, I had no idea. "He's waiting for you somewhere very different from here."

"Mutt" was all Checko said.

"You came looking for him in the last place you two were together and got stuck, that's all."

"I can hear him there," Checko said, his eyes rolling upward. "That's where he is. Far above this place. I think I see him."

"You *can* see him," I said, dizzy with encouragement. Or was it Faith? I couldn't say.

"I have to go now, young Julian," Checko said.

"All the years of nighttime, everything so many have seen…" I began.

"If I could help. Mutt would, too. But we can't."

There was frustration in his eyes.

"We're not a part of this."

He acknowledged Dr. Greer who was still studying the landscape of the mine walls with his back to us.

"Look to him. Look to The Lighted Man."

"Bring the tools."

Dr. Greer was in front of me, squinting over his shoulder into the glare of my wheat light.

The elevator was gone. Checko was nowhere in sight. The walls I'd seen Dr. Greer studying as I conversed with my phantom friend had been replaced by unfamiliar surroundings. A high pile of excavated dirt and rocks sat off to one side.

"*Julian!*"

"Uh, yeah. Yeah," I said from my gaping mouth.

Dr. Greer gave me a *Whassa-matter-you?* shrug.

"Get the tools." He wagged his finger at the canvas bag on the ground near my feet. "The tools."

I couldn't move. Where the hell were we? A second before, we were at the elevator shaft. Now...

"Didn't you see that? Didn't you just see what was going on?"

"What?!" Dr. Greer cried, jerking his head left to right as he ran up to me. "Where?!"

"Checko—I mean *Gino*—Muciarelli, he was right here, he was talking to me next to the elevator...." I drew a deep breath, lest I started to hyperventilate and pass out.

Grabbing me by my shoulders, Dr. Greer shook me violently, as if shaking dust from a rug as he yelled my name. I went limp in his grasp.

"The elevator is behind us!" he yelled. "We walked past it twenty minutes ago!" He gave me a final rough shake. "C'mon, stand up! It wasn't real!"

I grabbed onto him, hanging on for dear life and hoping to stop the sensation of falling I suddenly felt, falling from an impossible distance without end.

"*This* is real," he whispered, holding me tightly. He gave me a squeeze. "Buck up," he said into my ear. His hand held the back of my head on his shoulder. We stood there, locked together until my breathing slowed and I released a deep sigh. He pulled my head from his shoulder and looked me in the eyes.

"You okay?" he asked, wiping the sweat from my forehead before answering his own question. "You're okay." I could tell he was as freaked out as I was, but he forced a smile. "Whatever you see down here is the same as what you see up above. With one difference. Down here, time itself changes, at least as we know it. That's why we have to stay close. We have to stick together." He laid his hand on my cheek. "*This* is real." He took my hand in his, covering it with his other hand. "*This* is real." He turned me to face the dead-end of the tunnel. "*This* is what we have to break through. If we get separated down here, we run the risk of ending up like what I think is beyond this wall."

I didn't have to ask. He was talking about the thirty-five miners who were never recovered, trapped inside this foul black Hell for eternity.

Dr. Greer went to the wall and put his hands on his hips. "I've been chipping away at this goddamn wall for almost two years." He gave it a light kick and turned back around to me.

"You'd think I'd be—"

I took a step back as it happened.

"—through it by now—"

The top of the wall crumbled inward, leaving a knee-high hedgerow of rocks.

We both raised our arms to shield our faces against the stale exhalation of dust.

A black chasm revealed itself, refusing to be illuminated by our wheat-lights, as if the darkness beyond was a solid wall.

Dr. Greer turned to the newly revealed opening. Without hesitation, he stepped onto the stone hedgerow and leaned inside. "This is it," I heard him say into the stygian abyss.

Shuffling his feet on the stone ledge, he turned back to me. "How about that?" He broke into a smile, his face framed against the dark opening. "We're through."

Before I could respond, a half-dozen pale-green arms exploded from the darkness behind him, claw-like hands covering his face and pulling him backward into the opening.

Chapter Twelve
The Secret of David Sills

On any given day, Dan Gallo was the kind of man who expected supper to be on the table when he came home from his warehouse job. Moreover, he expected it to be something he wanted to eat. Never mind that his ever-changing palate gave no hint of his preference from day to day. That was his wife's job. In addition to keeping the house clean, Irene Gallo was expected to be a mind-reader. *Or else.*

Although Roger Gallo never actually verbalized the *or else* part when telling us this account of his father, it was always implied in the way his voice would trail off in a shunted whisper at the end of the story.

"Your Dad's a badass," Bill Purcell would affirm.

"Yeah, he's a great guy," Rayven and the rest of us would agree because it made Roger feel good and Roger was our friend.

The truth was the entire town of Harris knew that the elder Gallo was an abusive alcoholic and intolerant bigot where everybody but frustrated white male alcoholics were concerned. Dan Gallo was consumed with an obsessive hatred for not only strong women, so-called "non-white" persons, gay people, young people, "Hollywood-types", professional people, you name it, but also anyone else who dared to disagree with him on such pointless matters as *Ford vs. Chevy* or *paper vs. plastic*. Dan Gallo was simply a sad and frustrated man consumed with free-floating hatred for even his son's friends for the simple reason his son *had friends.*

Rayven understood this early on. He always stuck by Roger as his friend while correcting him at every turn when Roger would channel his father. Rayven forever saw the good in everyone he met and would strive to bring that goodness to light. It was his gift, the role of peacemaker.

I came to understand these social dynamics in a generalized, perhaps more primitive way. The effect was the same. I was able to step outside of my personal bubble of shame and embarrassment of being part of my family to comprehend one stark truth:

There is no such thing as a normal family.

Looking in from the outside and vice versa holds the same amount of deception for the observer.

I considered myself "different" because it was just me and my father.

For Roger, it was a tightrope he walked between love for his dad and the humiliation of being his son.

David Sills had a love-hate relationship with his parents' strict religiosity even though he considered it his own.

Bill Purcell had a stepdad whom he loved, at the same time wistfully pined for his biological father who had left when he was in the crib, started another family and wanted nothing to do with Bill and never would.

For Rayven, Evie, and Cami, it was Uncle Vincent's house.

Michael and Jean Woodruff in comparison, were by far the closest to "regular" parents, a forward-thinking and supportive couple to their daughter. But their household had its share of cobwebbed corners, too. For all their encouragement, Mr. and Mrs. Woodruff were blind to Casey's inner life and all the anxieties their daughter kept hidden deep inside herself.

No, there is no such thing as a "normal" family.

Neither is there such a thing as a "dysfunctional" family.

Good, bad, toxic, loving, supportive, broken, or abusive, rich or poor, it's the luck of the draw and you play the cards you're dealt as best as you can.

People from bad families can turn out good and people from good families can turn out horrid. At the end of the day, there's just family and we're all in those different situations with the same choices to consider, the same number of paths stretching before us. Each generation carries what they choose to carry into the future and there are many things to embrace or discard: Resentment. Hate. Love. Forgiveness. Secrets and lies or honesty and understanding. The choice was ours alone.

———

The Forester swerved back and forth down the trail, hitting saplings and threatening to plunge headlong off the side of Crumpton Hill as it sped willy-nilly over the dirt road, finally coming to rest on the gravel behind Pastore Lumber.

Dr. Greer threw open his door and jumped out, throwing his hands up to his face and pacing in front of the SUV. One of the headlights had been knocked out by the crazy descent, creating the illusion of the university professor appearing and disappearing as I looked out the windshield from the passenger seat.

Gently, I gripped the handle on my side and pulled up, letting the passenger-side door iris wide. After a beat, I threw my legs outside the vehicle, planting my feet on the ground and pulling the rest of my body from the Forester to a standing position.

"We broke through," I said numbly. "We were close to solving whatever's been happen—"

Dr. Greer stomped up to me and laughed in my face, so close I could taste his breath and feel drops of spittle dot my cheeks.

"*Close but no cigar!*" he shouted.

Chortling once more, he grabbed me by the front of my shirt collar with one hand.

"I'm not going back there!" he declared.

"Do you think I'm going back there?!" he asked.

"You saw what happened!" he declared. "Did you see what happened to me?!" he asked. "So much for my theory! So much for *its some energy from blah-blah-blah...* I don't know *ANYTHING*! Did you see those arms? Those goddamn dead stinky hands grabbed me by the head! *THE HEAD*!! Hey, I'm not going back there, I'm done, I'm—"

At that point, I did something I would have never considered doing to anyone, much less someone I thought of as a wizened adult.

I slapped Dr. Greer across the face.

Hard.

So hard his head spun sideways and he released his grip on my shirt.

So hard he buckled over and spun sideways, almost falling to his knees.

All I could see was his ass and doubled over backside as he growled *"YOU..."*

He straightened and whirled around to face me so fast that I stumbled backward in retreat but held my ground.

"You and I," he said. "We ain't going back there alone. Not anymore."

"But we can make it stop now," I tried. "We know how to make it stop once and for all."

Dr. Greer collapsed on the ground in a sitting position. He crossed his legs and put his hands in his lap. "How the hell did you do it? How did you pull me out?"

I shrugged. "I figured what was happening wasn't real. Just a shared vision, like you'd told me. I grabbed your pants at the waist and pulled you forward."

Dr. Greer blushed. "And I ran."

"We *both* ran. We saw the same thing. Only you felt it. I just followed you out."

"I'm done with this, Mr. Baker. This is stronger than any two people."

The moon shone brightly over the lumberyard, casting dancing shadows around our glowing faces.

I plopped down on the gravel opposite him, staring into his eyes in earnest. "What if we can get a group of people to go back down there?"

"A kind of posse," Dr. Greer tried.

I nodded. "Leave it to me."

———————

Autumn sprang full-blown at the end of September. The dual-victory of the salami and cheese-wheel enjoyed by me and Rayven was all but forgotten. Even my weekend adventure with Casey Woodruff and the Play-Doh head faded into a distant memory.

But the underlying mystery of it all; the hill, the house, the coal mine, all surrounded by ever-evolving visions, remained at the forefront of my attention. I felt closer to the recently frenetic Dr. Harlan Greer—he of the previously even-tempered and stalwart college professor—than I did my own father. And now I had the mission to gather a group of people to join us in revisiting the dangerous tunnels of the shuttered mine.

Rayven was in, agreeing before I'd even finished my pitch. We'd been partners-in-crime since elementary school, so finding out the truth about my slumber party at his house, about me and Casey and what we saw and how we met Dr. Greer elicited only a slight nod, as if he'd heard it all before.

"I'll get some guys," he said without hesitation. "No problem."

Two days later, on Wednesday—*hump day*, no less—I opened my locker and tossed my books inside as the school day came to end. As I slammed the door closed, a folded piece of paper tumbled like a feather to the floor in front of my feet. I picked it up and studied the closed locker in front of me. It must have been wedged half-in/half-out of one of the four louvered slots on the locker door, I reasoned. I unfolded the paper, my eyes narrowing to read the handwritten note:

Dear Julian, I'm sorry. Please don't hate me.

The note was signed *Casey W.*

Underneath the name was a phone number.

Underneath the phone number was a Smiley face replacing the standard *P.S.*, followed by the words *Call me.*

Walking home, wearing a smile the entire way, I kept patting the outside of my jeans pocket, the crinkle of paper inside a constant reassurance that Casey's note was real. It was the next best feeling to walking beside her and holding her hand. I strutted down the uneven sidewalk, gazing up in wonder at the changing leaves on the elm and maple trees lining the street as if seeing them for the first time.

My steps hastened to a slow trot. I wanted to get home and call Casey as fast as I could, before the trail grew cold, so to speak.

The thought crossed my mind to send her a text message, to communicate with her as Dr. Greer and I had done, but it was a fleeting and silly notion. Although I had my own cell phone, a clumsy *flip-phone* affair that was obsolete the minute it came out, I was the only one of my friends who had such a device as far as I knew. Dad gifted me the phone out-of-the-blue one day to use between us for any rare emergencies that might come up. Never fond of the thing, it *had* come in handy for communicating with Dr. Greer. Every household in town including ours had landlines and push-button telephones which I was told was a welcome relief from the "old" rotary phones, whatever they were.

Answering machines were a luxury I hadn't yet heard of. There was no Caller ID; you just answered the phone with a bright greeting of *"Hello!"* On the other end of the line, it was always someone you knew, unlike the telemarketers and scammers inundating landlines and cell phones alike today. Sure, several people in Harris carried the new technology of cellular-based telephonic convenience in their pockets at the time. But when I look back, as old-fashioned as landlines seem today, they were always steady and reliable. Besides, people found it way better to socialize with someone while looking them in the eye.

My position on the burgeoning technology would shift and mature as the days turned into years, but on that day with Casey's handwritten note in my jeans pocket, I walked with a bop in my step and a simple old-fashioned anticipation for what would come next. When I finally reached home, went inside, and dialed the Woodruff's phone number, who would answer?

Casey's mom?

Casey's dad?

Or Casey herself *(could I dare to hope)*?

After that, what would I say? Rehearsed or not, would I stumble over my words when the phone was answered and the Fates called *"ACTION!?"* Or would I be the smooth-talking "Mr. Charm" I hoped to be? Although filled with anxiety and a bundle of nerves, the variables, and potential outcomes of making the call were nothing but thrilling in a good way.

In that same way, what happened with David Sills could have turned out very differently.

He could have sent me a text I'd have either put off or outright ignored.

As it turned out, I cut right off the sidewalk into the grass and jogged into my front yard, slowing to a stop in the middle of the lawn at the sight of David sitting on the stoop outside the front door. He smiled and gave me a friendly wave, which I returned despite my sudden frustration at his intrusion. My plan was to immediately call Casey's house but for the unexpected presence of David Sills! Of all people! pretty much screwed that up. Still, in an uncharacteristic fashion for me, I took a deep breath and resolved to be patient.

"David!" I called, forcing a smile. "What're you doing here?"

He immediately apologized, asking if it was a bad time.

I shook my head. "Nah. Just surprised to see you," I said, which I most certainly was. This was the first time David had ever been to my house. I didn't think he even knew where I lived. I liked him okay, insofar as I thought about him at all. Our interactions in school had been marginal at best, and only when Rayven was present. Rayven, after all, was his champion of sorts, and knew him better than anyone else in our circle of friends. As I came up to him, I saw his cheeks were red as beets. I knelt in front of him, trying to act casual.

"Everything okay?" I asked.

"Sure," David nodded. "Everything's okay. Just wanted to come by and hang out. Maybe talk a little."

I flashed the peace sign. "That's cool."

The presence of David Sills on my doorstep went from inconvenience to opportunity at light-speed. If I played my cards right, I could enlist him in the posse and therefore convince Dr. Greer to return to the Black Diamond Mine.

I stepped past him and opened the front door. He stood up and faced me as I gestured through the open doorway. "We can hang out in my room," I offered.

He returned my peace sign with one of his own. "Perfect."

Where Dad was, I had no idea. In his bedroom sleeping or not home at all, it didn't matter either way.

To my surprise, David went immediately to a copy of *Famous Monsters of Filmland* lying on the floor as he stepped into my room. He went to his knees in front of the magazine and picked it up.

"Wow," he breathed, marveling at the cover. "Christopher Lee as Dracula!" He picked it up and cradled it between both hands, careful not to bend the pages of the front and back covers as he studied the image of Lee's blood-shot eyes and fanged visage. David smiled as if he were alone.

"You like the Hammer films, huh? Me, too."

David put the magazine back on the floor.

"You can look at it," I said. "I have a bunch of other *Famous Monsters* and comics. You can check 'em all out."

He kept staring at the cover of *Famous Monsters of Filmland* at his knees. "I *love* the Hammer films," he whispered. "I wish I could see more, like *The Gorgon* and *Curse of Frankenstein*."

"Oh, they're great—" I began, then stopped. I didn't want to gush about things such as the movies and magazines his parents would never allow him to see. At the same time, I wondered how he knew about such things. So, I asked him.

David's answer revealed more in three words than most books.

"I sneak out."

I was intrigued by the intrigue, so I pressed him.

"You sneak out?"

"All the time," he answered. After a heavy sigh, he added, "*Well*…when I can."

I didn't know how to answer, so I said "Yeah, I know how that goes."

David cocked his head at me. "*Do* you? Hm. Never figured your dad for a religious fanatic."

And then he smiled. The joke was on me.

"I've sat in the back of the Palace Theater watching so many movies with one eye on the screen and one eye on the doors, waiting for my parents to appear and drag me out, you wouldn't believe."

David was easy to talk to; as afternoon turned to evening, I began to understand Rayven's solid loyalty to him since elementary school. When I told him about Dr. Greer and the Black Diamond Mine and how Rayven and I were searching for reliable friends to join our expedition, he immediately agreed.

"I'm in. Even if I have to fight past my folks to run out the front door. You guys have been putting up with all that stuff long enough."

"I'm sure Rayven's going to ask Gallo to come with us," I confessed, mentioning David's tormentor.

"That's okay. Maybe he can insult all the creepy shit down there into going away."

My mouth went slack. After a beat, I burst out laughing. "I can't believe you just said *shit*!"

"Yeah," David agreed with a quiet chuckle. His voice grew serious. "I can't believe Rayven never told me about that himself."

"I don't think he's ever told anyone. I just found out about what's been happening a few weeks ago. He had a hard time telling *me* about it. We got drunk at the Little Italy Festival a few hours after we saw you and rode the tractor. He told me after we drank a bunch of beers."

"So many secrets. Everyone has 'em, I guess. Some worse than others." He was talking to himself out loud it seemed, eyes staring unfocused and trance-like, fixated on something beyond me and my room, looking past the walls at something only he could see.

"What do you mean?" I asked, knowing full well what he meant. Casey Woodruff was my secret. Maybe she was ignoring me in public because I was her secret. Uncle Vincent and Aunt Laurie had secrets of their own. I was surrounded by subterfuge, including my own self-deceptions and doubts. It was a lonely feeling. Lonely and sad and very frightening.

"I don't have many friends except for your cousin. I know you guys are close. You're like brothers." David said.

I nodded. "I'm your friend, too, David."

He continued as if he didn't hear me. "I thought, *It's Senior Year. Pretty soon I'll graduate and this will all be behind me so I should just keep my head down and my mouth shut for a little while longer,* but I can't do it. I just can't do it anymore. I don't see Rayven much beyond school and there was no way I was going to him in a hallway between classes or at lunch and I wasn't going to call him, to talk to him on the phone. All I could picture was him hanging up."

"I don't understand," I said, leaning forward with narrowed eyes.

Again, David didn't acknowledge my confusion. "So, I decided last night to come here after school today and talk to you. I've always thought you were a good guy."

I couldn't stand it anymore. I grabbed David's arms, giving them a single shake. "*David,*" I urged with as much calm and earnest as I could muster.

We locked eyes.

"I'm going to get up and leave after this, I promise. I'll just get up and go away, just so you know."

"David," I repeated. I was more confused than ever. All I wanted to do was make him feel safe and reassured, no matter what. Whether it was the imploring look on my face or something else, David took a deep breath. What he said next I've come to realize was a reserve of the strongest example of courage I've ever witnessed.

"I'm gay, Julian. I've known I was gay since the third grade."

I let go of his arms, leaned back against my heels, and released a deep sigh. "*Man!* You had me freaked out for a second."

Now it was David's turn to look confused. It was all he could do as I continued.

"You're gay. So what? *Man!* I thought you were gonna tell me you were dying or something!"

He was incredulous. "It doesn't matter?"

I was on a roll, relieved as I could be. "Yeah, it matters! That you don't have some kind of terminal illness, that you're not fucking dying! Of course, it matters! You scared me half to death and back again, man!"

David's body melted, going from a tightly coiled garage door spring to a relaxed pile of neatly folded freshly washed towels. All tension he'd been carrying for God-knows-how long seemed to vanish in a second.

"This is between us," I assured him. "You and me, *period.* I can tell you right now that Rayven would feel the same way I do, but I'll never say anything to him or anyone else. That's your call, Dave. I respect that."

"Thanks, Julian. I appreciate that more than you know. I'm not sure what I'll do yet." The faraway look returned to his eyes for a moment. "My family would probably throw me into the Wabash River if they knew. Mom, Dad, my brothers, and sisters. They'd haul the gunnysack with me inside and heave it into the current never thinking they'd done anything wrong and jabbering their speaking-in-tongues nonsense all the while."

"Dad always told me religion is nothing but mental poison."

"It can be," he said. "Your dad's right," he continued. "But I believe Jesus Christ is my Savior. He died for my sins and forgave me, thousands of years before I was ever born. So right now, I'm okay. I've been forgiven by Jesus. I'm a whole person, same as you and everyone else, whether anyone else believes that or not."

I glanced at the copy of *FM #84* between us, Christopher Lee's Dracula-face staring at me upside-down. I didn't know what to do with my hands, so I put one hand on my leg and reached out to him with the other hand.

All I could say was, "I agree." And I meant it.

We shook hands and exchanged mutual smiles.

Then we hugged tightly, two friends against the shifting tides of the world.

Unfortunately, my talk with Casey didn't go as well. After David had left, I rang her number. First, her mother answered. After I asked in a constricted voice if Casey was there, her mother asked who was calling. I mumbled I was a friend from school. Silence. Then Casey's voice stabbed my ear with a curt *"Hello?"*

Although her voice softened after discovering it was me, she made it clear in no uncertain terms that there was no way things would change at school and no way *in hell* could we ever see each other outside of the neat parameters of school hallways ever again and that it was her choice. As a consolation, she said she was sorry she'd ignored me in school, but it had to be that way. When I confronted her about the note she left me, about what it meant, she said it was an apology, nothing more and now she had apologized again and there was nothing more to be said. Before she could end the call, I stopped her. "The other thing in your note," I said, finishing before she could respond.

"I could never hate you."

Chapter Thirteen

Once More Unto the Breach, Dear Friends

Putting the logistics together was simple enough: Our cover story was that everyone was going to the football game that Friday. Instead of going home, Rayven would hang out with Bill Purcell. The two of them would meet up with Roger Gallo. The three of them would meet me and David Sills at my house. Using Dad's Jeep to ostensibly transport the five of us to the game, I'd actually drive up Crumpton Hill to the mine opening where Dr. Greer would be waiting for us. We'd go in under his tutelage around 4:30 in the afternoon and solve the two-generations-old mystery, returning home around the same time the game would end between 10:30 and 11:00 that night. *No sweat.*

During the Friday lunch period, everyone agreed to the plan and was sworn to secrecy. Barring the most extreme of unforeseen circumstances, in seven days we'd all be descending into the mine. All we had to do was finish breaking through to find the bodies of the lost miners. Once that happened, their restless spirits could at last find peace and the phenomenon of nightly visions over Crumpton Hill would finally come to an end. *No sweat.*

Saturday morning

I woke before Dad, as usual when he had no weekend gig. Dad slept late on his off days, meaning Mondays through Thursdays. Absent a gig, he stayed up doing God-knows-what until all hours, rarely waking before noon or after. Dad came out of his bedroom a little before noon, all janky and coughing, holding a lit cigarette. I was watching *Ricochet* on Netflix. He plopped down beside me on the couch and cleared his throat with a sharp *hrrk!*

"Denzel Washington," he said. "Can't go wrong."

Dad was a true unsung movie aficionado. In another life he could have been Robert Osborne or any number of film historians. I knew what was coming, so I remained silent. I'd heard the monologue many times before that he was about to soliloquize yet again:

"There is no other actor—and I mean *no other actor*—with that man's skill. Look at *Falling, He Got Game, Philadelphia*—you name it! Watching Denzel Washington's performances...he elevates every movie he's in..."

Here it comes—

"...and the Academy Awards ignore him for *years*, until he finally wins the Oscar for—"

Wait for it—

"—*Training Day!* Hey, that was a great movie, don't get me wrong. But I gotta think that, given all his other performances in the years leading up to that win, he had to be like '*For this one? Okay, no problem. About fucking time.*'"

"Can I use the Jeep to go to the football game on Friday?"

Dad stubbed out his cigarette in the ashtray on the coffee table and went *hrrk!* again. "This coming Friday? Yeah, sure. They shoulda given him the goddamn Oscar for *this* movie. Or *Devil in a Blue Dress. GLORY, for Chrissakes!*"

Sunday afternoon

I've always hated Sundays. That was the day that marked the end of the weekend, the day that began with a creeping anxiety of what awaited at school the following morning. Friday nights blazed with anticipation and excitement. Then Saturday would arrive to usher in the familiar euphoria of having reached a fleeting Shangri-La promising to last forever. Then the sun would rise on Sunday morning. To put it another way: Friday was driving to Disney World. Saturday was living in Disney World. Sunday was saying goodbye to a magic you never wanted to end; Sunday was driving back.

Around 3:30, I decided against my better judgment to call Casey again.

This time, her father answered and I repeated my nervous verbal tap-dance, bracing myself for Casey's razor-sharp greeting. Instead, this happened:

"Julian! *What* is going on?!"

"I just wanted to talk to you."

"Don't give me that *shit*. Cami says Rayven is acting weird, says him and a bunch of guys are planning *something big*, he says. She's freaked out."

"How would, I mean, why would, you know, what the hell do I have to do with…with whatever Rayven…I don't know what you're talking about."

"Yes, you do, Julian Baker, *yes you do*. Don't you dare lie to me."

"Oh, okay, *Mom*. How dare I lie to you, right, *Mom?* You and I went through more in two nights than any *ten* people go through in a lifetime, but what does that matter now, huh? *Huh?!* You said it yourself! Can't talk to you in the halls, Julian! Can't acknowledge you so much as exist, Julian! That's the way it's gotta be, Julian! Now you're all shocked that I *dare* lie to you! I got news for you, kid, you're *not* my mother. My mother's dead. You hear me? She's *dead!* I can lie to you up one side and down the other and you can't do nuthin' about it. We were gonna figure this out together but now you're on your own, you understand me?!"

"Julian, I'm scared."

"Yeah, well, join the club! Sorry I called you the first time!"

I slammed the phone down so hard, the ghost ring's echo trilled from the innards of the landline, filling the air after the call ended. The word *bitch* rang inside my head, over and over. I stomped into my bedroom, slamming the door hard enough to throw the posters on my wall out of level to hang at crazy crooked angles. Throwing myself onto the bed, I buried my face into the pillow and lay there sobbing with rage until my anger ebbed, flowing into frustration, then self-pity. By five 'o clock, I cried myself to sleep for the rest of the day.

———————

The next four days passed slowly, hours dripping tediously away like molasses. We ate our lunches in silence, never talking about what might be awaiting us on Friday. It was like we were all lost inside fog-shrouded cocoons, alone with our personal thoughts. And personal demons, as well. Even though there was a group of us committed to the same goal, I felt more alone and lost than ever. I hadn't caught so much as a glimpse of Casey in school the whole week.

Friday finally arrived, a day filled with sunshine and unusually warm weather. A good sign, I thought. During the day, each of us exchanged knowing nods as we passed in the hallways. At lunch, Bill Purcell said he was bringing a bunch of flares and some rope, along with assorted hand tools, salt pills, and a camera. No one, not even Roger Gallo, gave him the business about the salt pills and camera. Instead, we expressed unanimous approval at his choice of supplies. The rest of the school day passed quickly; my confidence restored after what had been the longest four days of my life.

"I didn't bring near as much as Bill," David confessed as we walked to my house.

"What, no camera?" I asked with mock seriousness.

Reaching into his jeans pocket, David produced a pocket Bible. "I brought this."

Throwing my arm over his shoulder, I gave him a quick pull to me before letting him go. "It sure can't hurt," I assured him.

144

David smiled. "Better than salt pills."

————————————

We'd been sitting on the stoop outside my front door for about twenty minutes when Rayven, Roger and Bill appeared. They were in lockstep, three abreast, sauntering down the sidewalk like gunslingers.

Only Roger Gallo appeared different: he was dressed in loose-fitting jungle camouflage with a bulging field pack attached to his back. All that was missing was a combat helmet and an M-16 slung over his shoulder.

David and I looked at each other.

"I'm not going to say anything."

Nodding, I said, "Me neither."

G.I. Joe. Rambo. Total asshole.

"Didn't say a word."

"Me neither," I repeated.

We all greeted one another and started to pile into the Jeep when Bill Purcell blurted out, "Let's get rich!"

Rayven's shoulders sank. "Okay, Bill!" He gave me a nervous laugh. "Give us a second," he said to the others. He took my arm, ushering me around the house to the backyard as I glared at him.

Once out of earshot and view of the guys, I hissed "Let's get rich? *Let's get rich?!*"

Rayven backed me up against the house. "Okay, okay, let me explain this."

Staring daggers at him, I tilted my head. "Please do."

"Okay, okay. Look, I didn't tell them *exactly* what we're doing."

"Oh, you didn't tell them—what exactly *did* you tell them?"

Rayven looked down at his shuffling feet. "Well, you know, the mine-thing, going down into the mine, they know all about that."

"Keep going."

"So, you know, the dangers of going into the mine and everything, they know all about that, so, okay."

145

"Rayven," I said as calmly as possible, "what do they think they're about to do?"

"They're here, okay? They're with us."

"No, no, no." This couldn't be happening. I took Rayven gently by the arms, resisting the urge to shake him violently. "I told David everything. I told him the truth. What did you tell Roger and Bill?"

Rayven couldn't look me in the eye. "I told them about the gold."

"The gold? *What gold?*"

"I told them there was a buncha gold in the mine and that if we could bring it out, we'd split it and all be rich."

I balled my right hand into a fist and put it under his chin. I was shaking so hard, I thought I'd come out of my shoes.

Rayven closed his eyes. "I know, I know. I was scared to tell them. But we needed them and they're here. They're ready to go in with us."

I couldn't argue with that. Rayven had lived with the stigma of living in Uncle Vincent's house his whole life. I'd just found out about that curse a few weeks ago. I couldn't fault him. He was right.

I opened the fist and laid the hand on his shoulder.

"Are *you* ready?"

Rayven looked up at me through tear-filled eyes, saying "I've *been* ready, *cuz*. For a long time."

Pressing my forehead to his, I said, "Then let's go, man."

———————

The town seemed different, somehow older and less appealing than it did two short months ago. The Jeep rolled over desolate streets past silent and shuttered homes. There were no families walking on crowded sidewalks on their way to watch a parade or join the revelries at the fairgrounds along the Wabash River. There were no tractors roaring over the asphalt filled with happy people. The Wine Garden was dark and abandoned, hibernating until almost a year from now when it would once again reawaken. Harris had become a foreboding ghost town full of hidden secrets behind each lighted window in the homes we passed. I pulled in behind Pastore Lumber, steering the Jeep to the bottom of Crumpton Hill and slamming on the brakes.

Casey stepped out from the tree line into the middle of the gravel road. Dressed in knee-high buckle-boots and all black, she looked every bit as terrifying as any phantasm. She was ready to take on the world, starting with us.

From the passenger seat, Rayven said, *"I'll hop in the back."*

Casey climbed into the Jeep without saying a word, staring straight ahead.

I gunned the Jeep up Crumpton Hill. An instant later, I felt the gentle squeeze of Casey's hand on my leg. Placing my hand atop hers, the six of us continued our ascent up the narrow gravel lane until we reached the mine opening and Dr. Greer's parked Forester. I pulled alongside it and checked the time on the dashboard before killing the engine. *4:45pm.*

Casey looked over at me, her eyes wide and searching. The expression on her face told me what no amount of words ever could. Everything coming before suddenly fell away, as if a veil lifted from my eyes. I gripped her hand so hard in mine, I thought she would wince. Instead, she raised her chin and gave me her best tight-lipped smile under dark eyes. At that moment, I knew we were both equally scared yet confident. *Do or die*, I thought, almost hearing her answer: *Do.*

The vacant handcar waited at the opening of the mine. Dr. Greer was nowhere in sight.

Everyone climbed from the Jeep and began milling around. I took advantage of the opportunity to ask Casey how she knew to meet us behind Pastore Lumber when she had.

"Rayven told me Tuesday at school," she said.

At that moment Rayven walked up to us.

"Did you tell her about the gold?" I asked with a wink.

Rayven blushed and Casey gave me a sideways glance.

"Never mind," Rayven and I said in unison.

David, Bill, and Roger were peering through the windows of the Forester.

"Where's your guy?" David hollered over to me.

I shook my head, scanning the surroundings. Except for us, the place was quiet and deserted. Over my shoulder, a voice boomed with surprise:

"*Whoa!* Thought they'd called out the National Guard!"

Roger Gallo was standing just inside the mine's entrance. A few feet further inside stood Dr. Greer. I watched as he and Roger shook hands.

Dr. Greer stepped past Roger, emerging into the open. Catching sight of me and Casey, he flashed a wide-mouthed grin of recognition and a quick wave. "Mr. Baker!" Closing the distance between us with wide strides, he stopped abruptly in front of us. Extending a hand to Casey, instead of shaking it, he took her hand in his palm, bowed, and planted a light kiss on her knuckles. "And Ms. Woodruff. Lovely as ever."

He straightened, rotating on his heels to look everyone over before turning back to me with an approving nod. "You brought an army."

I introduced him to Rayven and Dr. Greer shook his hand with vigor. "The *other* Mr. Baker! Vincent's son. *Very* nice to meet you!"

"Yes, sir," Rayven said, taken aback by the man's animated demeanor. "Thank you."

"And these three fine gentlemen?"

I introduced David and Bill and Roger. Dr. Greer shook each of their hands in turn.

Motioning us to the back of the Forester, he popped the rear door and handed each of us mini walkie-talkies and hard hats equipped with wheat lights.

Bill Purcell opened his backpack and took out what looked like a shoebox. "I've got flares," he announced.

Dr. Greer regarded him in silence for a moment before saying, "That's good. But we must be careful with open flame or sparks of any kind. A lot of combustible dust where we're going, you know?" He took the box from Bill and stuffed it into his own backpack. "Better let me hang onto these." He gave Bill a pat on the shoulder. "Good thinking," he said diplomatically. "They might very well come in handy."

Bill beamed at us. "I've got a camera, too."

"A camera's fine," Dr. Greer said to the group. "Anyone else have any matches, lighters, anything that flames or sparks?"

We all shook our heads. Dr. Greer focused on Roger, who'd been unusually quiet since he'd arrived at my house.

"What about you? No flints or whetstones, things like that?"

"Nothing," Roger answered.

"Good!" He clapped his hands, the sound making us jump. We followed him over to the handcar. Standing in front of it, the dark opening of the mine at his back, he delivered a speech in a high-pitched voice.

"Before we go down inside here, I want to tell you that you're apt to see some pretty strange things."

I had to stifle a laugh. It reminded me of Luther Heggs, Don Knotts' character in *The Ghost and Mr. Chicken.*

"It's crucial that we stick together. Nothing any of us may see can do us any *actual* harm if we don't get separated. We're going down to a dig a couple hundred feet underground, give or take a couple hundred feet. I've been working on this for a long time. This dig needs to be vented outside of the mine to release certain energies that have been building up for half a century. It's my contention that this energy is searching for a way out, it wants to dissipate. It wants to be free."

Bill Purcell started to raise his hand, but I stopped him with an outstretched arm.

"Consider a trapped animal," Dr. Greer continued. "A trapped animal is not only frightened, but also *frightening*. It thrashes against its cage, gnashing its jaws, showing its fangs, doing *anything it can* to intimidate its perceived enemies, even those who wish to render aid to the animal."

"What about the gold?" Bill hissed at me.

I gave Rayven a *goddamn you* look. He shrugged.

Dr. Greer heard Bill's question. "Good question, young man," he said without missing a beat. "Any gold you find is yours to keep."

Bill pumped his hand with a triumphant "*Yesss!*"

"After you get past all the monsters," Dr. Greer added.

"Wait. *What?!*"

Roger punched his arm. "Shut up, moron."

Dr. Greer pointed at me. "Mr. Baker knows the drill about the handcar, knows where we're going and knows what to expect. If you get separated from me, make sure you know where he is. Again, we should all try to stick together. Our only goal is to vent the dig to the outside world, outside of the mine. Is everyone ready?"

We surged forward a few steps into the mine, turning on our wheat lights. "We're ready," I said.

"Miss Woodruff will remain topside with the handcar. She'll monitor our communications over the walkies and be ready to send it down for us if needed." He gave Casey a hopeful look, but she was having none of it.

"Like hell I will." She leaned forward, hands firmly on hips. "I'm going down with the rest of you."

Dr. Greer furrowed his brow. "Hmm."

"Let one of these *boys* babysit the handcar," she said, specifically glaring at Roger Gallo. Gallo gave her the finger.

"Hmm." Dr. Greer was reevaluating the situation. I could almost see the wheels of thought as he weighed the options.

I was frozen, not sure where I stood. On the one hand Casey would probably be safer staying up here. Then again, she would be alone. All I could do was watch what was happening play out.

Casey responded to Gallo, giving *him* the finger. "Back at you, you pig-faced bully motherfu—"

"*Okay!*" Dr. Greer shouted, clapping his hands once. "We can't all fit on the handcar anyway—" He clapped his hands again. "Great idea, Miss Woodruff!"

Casey flashed us an angelic, satisfied smile. Dr. Greer pumped his fist into the yawning black opening.

"Onward!"

The second time going into the Black Diamond Coal Mine was nothing like the first. This time was more relaxed, less an expedition and more like a tour surrounded by a group of friends. Flanked by Rayven and Casey, I moved forward with confident steps, looking back every so often at the entrance still illuminated by daylight.

David, directly behind us, was fascinated by the environment of decrepitude existing side-by-side with the ease of our journey.

Bill Purcell and Roger Gallo took up the rear. They walked in silence. Only the wheat lights, flashing over the walls and ceiling let us know they were behind us.

In front of us, Dr. Greer's wheat light pierced the darkness, casting flickering shadows in rhythm with his steps. He hummed absently under his breath, the impromptu melody taking on eerie echoes the farther we descended. The lighted archway of the entrance behind us grew smaller and smaller until it disappeared completely. My body tensed, but I was surrounded by friends this time. I had already seen where we were going and now, I knew what we were going to do, unlike that first time.

No sweat, I repeated to myself.

As we walked next to the iron tracks curving deeper down into the mine, I noticed things I hadn't seen the first time I'd come down with Dr. Greer. There had been my experience at the elevator, but other than that, we'd walked a simple dirt path to the excavation.

Now, the true nature of the mine revealed itself in my wheat light.

The mine was shored up with frames of timber running along the walls and over the ceiling. Once fresh and true, now the wood, blackened with coal dust, was decayed and warped and missing altogether in many places. The air was choked, stagnant. With each step, the ancient filth covered my shoes and crawled up my jeans to the knee. The skin of my face was tight with foul dust. Sweat gathering under my helmet crawled over my forehead and down my cheeks like swamp mud. When I heard Bill Purcell whisper from behind, "This sucks," I couldn't disagree. This was no place to leave one's ghost. This was Hell right here on Earth.

Growing up as I had, I never considered myself religious in the least nor particularly concerned with the afterlife. From as far back as memory allowed, it was me and Dad. Not so much father and son as adult and child roommates. Dad did the best he could as a parent, which was considerable given our circumstances, and I respected and followed the guidance he provided. But there was an easy air between us; we helped each other in our way. Sometimes it seemed *I* was the adult to the child. Dad was gentle and kind. He was worldly and intelligent and well-spoken. But he was also lost and given to dark moods of self-doubt and despair. This was where I came in. I was not so much his crutch as his anchor to a fondly remembered, yet forlorn past. He taught me that an open flame could burn me horribly if I thrust a bare hand into the fire. He taught me to look both ways before stepping into the street. He taught me about the loyalty and love one person can share with another and he warned me about disappointment and loss, steeling me against regret and surrender though he had given up his personal battle against those things long ago. In that way, Dad was like the thirty-five dead miners we had come down here to offer release. They were trapped in a forgotten stygian Purgatory. Even though Dad was above ground, he, too, was trapped in the dark chasms of his own mind. Maybe we all were like the miners and Dad. Rayven, Cami, and Evie, along with Uncle Vincent and Aunt Laurie, living lives stunted by their secret. David Sills, constricted by the confusion of a religion foisted upon him by his parents, neither of which he understood. Was it any different for Bill or Roger or Casey? For Harlan Greer, a doctor and credentialed academic?

According to his theory, thirty-five lost souls sought to escape the trap fate had sprung on them two generations ago. Was anyone else any different? The question came to a full-stop inside my head. I took a few quick steps away from Rayven and Casey to catch up with Dr. Greer, to ask him a simple question.

"Why are you doing this?"

"Say what now?" asked Dr. Greer.

"You're obsessed," I blurted. "There's something. I don't know."

As we continued our slow shuffle, Dr. Greer moved close enough that our shoulders rubbed as we walked so he could focus his words on my left ear. "I knew you were a smart guy the first time we met."

"You've been doing this for a long time. Not for any recognition."

He stopped and raised his hand. Turning around, he told everyone to wait. Then, he took my arm and we walked several feet ahead of the others.

"Two people are going about their day. It's an average, normal day, same as a hundred days before. I mean *exactly* the same. Whether working in a mine, or a school or a restaurant, or driving the same route for the hundredth time, it's a routine. *It's familiar. It's safe.* Until suddenly, it's not safe. Until suddenly, a young mother and her four-year-old child cross paths with a night-shift stocker at a grocery store who needs that final blast of meth to get him home after a long night. Two totaled cars, three dead, countless people left behind to grieve."

A light went off inside my head.

"You're looking for your family."

I was taken aback by his sympathetic, yet somehow patronizing smile. "*No*," said Dr. Greer. "My family is long gone. They left years ago on a gravel road three states east of here."

"Then why?"

Dr. Greer looked left and right, trying to avoid my question. He sighed deeply. "I've lived in a lot of places. An occupational hazard for college professors. This is the only place I've found where certain paths cross. I tried to explain this to your dad and uncle when I tried to buy this ground. They thought of it as something to keep quiet about, their personal curse to bear for reasons they never explained."

My grandparents. Dad and Vincent had seen the images of their dead parents. This, after growing up with conflicted relationships between them, with a mother and father who tried to turn brother against brother. Or so the brothers thought. And so, the brothers resisted, vowing to stick together after their parents had died. Which they had.

It had all been a lie. What Vincent and John Baker had seen that night at the edge of the woods was NOT their parents. It was a cry for help from thirty-five trapped souls screaming for the attention of anyone who might be able to help them reach whatever place they knew they needed to be. Whether it's called Heaven or Utopia or Shangri-La, I don't know.

"This is where the ghosts are," said Dr. Greer. "In this horrible place. I'm here to honor the dead. To help both them and the living. That's why I'm here." He paused in his typical fashion before adding, "That, and to teach, of course. This equipment doesn't pay for itself." He signaled the others and we continued our descent.

———————

What to make of the esteemed Dr. Harlan Greer? I'd taken to him that night in the woods when we first met, though I didn't quite know why then. It was something, a familiar yet indefinable feeling one gets from a first impression. Sometimes, you come away not liking someone for similar intuitive reasons impossible to put into words. When it came to me, I almost stumbled into Casey.

Dr. Greer had lost his family. I had lost my mother. *Kindred spirits.* I felt like Dr. Greer was a kindred spirit. The feeling was so strong I'd lied to visit him at the University and lied once more to follow him into the Black Diamond Mine. Now, I'd not only lied a third time to return with him, but I'd also recruited most of the people I cared about to follow me back down into this filthy hole to pursue his far-fetched theory.

What if Dr. Greer was wrong? Horrible things roamed inside these constricted tunnels, of that there was no doubt. But what if, instead of releasing such a concentration of energy that manifested above ground as furtive phantoms, we were about to unleash full-blown monsters whose goals weren't to find peace, but to wreak havoc? What if both Dr. Greer and I had been so blinded by our own losses that we were unable to understand our intentions would turn out to be fatally misguided?

I stopped short of thinking, *We're all about to die* (even though the thought did cross my mind) and hollered to Dr. Greer who had moved well ahead of us.

"We're almost to the elevator shaft!" he yelled back.

I turned around. The wheat light flashed across Casey's face and came to rest on the pale faces of David Sills and Bill Purcell.

"Where's Rayven and Gallo?" I said with sudden panic.

They didn't need to speak. The terror in their eyes said it all.

Chapter Fourteen

35 Skidoo

"They were just here!"

"They were right behind us!"

"Where'd they go?!" I screamed.

"I didn't see anything!"

"You *had* to see something!" Casey yelled, grabbing hold of my arm.

David said as calmly as he could. "They just *weren't here* anymore."

Dr. Greer came running. "What's going on?!"

"We've lost Rayven and Roger!" I hollered.

"What do you mean *lost?!*" Dr. Greer snapped. "I told you guys to stick together! *Stick together*, I said!" He shouted Rayven's name twice. "*Guys!*" he tried once more. There was no answer.

"We were together," Bill Purcell cried. "I want to get out of here."

David turned up his palms, pleading with me. "They were just *gone*. Rayven was right behind me. He said it sure was dusty and I said I had water in my backpack. I heard him say, 'That sounds great.' I pulled my backpack off and turned around and he and Roger were gone."

I looked down at the backpack at David's feet, then back up at David.

"*Just gone*," David whispered.

Bill Purcell was on his knees. "We stuck together," he sobbed. "Goddamnit, we stuck together. Goddamnit."

156

Casey and David took him by the arms and hauled him to his feet. Dr. Greer stepped up to him nodding encouragement.

"I know you did, son."

Bill sniffled, swallowing a wad of saliva and releasing a deep breath. "I'm ready to go home now."

"I know you are," Dr. Greer said. He patted Bill's cheek. "Keep breathing. Take some deep breaths."

I took a bottle of water from David's backpack, twisted off the plastic cap and offered it to Bill. He drank greedily, downing most of the bottle before coming up for air to thank me. "It's dark down here. It's like being awake and asleep at the same time."

Dr. Greer studied Bill's face, wiping the tears from his cheeks and looking into his eyes. "Let's all take a break," he urged Bill. "Sound good?" Bill nodded and Dr. Greer motioned with his index finger for David and Casey to let him go. We all kneeled in a circle on the ground.

"Okay, look," Dr. Greer said, his eyes focused on the ground. "There are offshoots on either side of us. These other tunnels, these veins, aren't very long and all lead to dead ends." He tapped a finger in the dirt. "*This* is the main chute from top to bottom, from where we started to the point of the explosion. We're more than halfway to the point of the explosion, where we need to be. We're almost there."

"No way. I'm not gonna leave Rayven."

"Of course not," Dr. Greer said to me. "We're not leaving anybody."

"So, then. What now?" asked Casey.

Dr. Greer thought a moment before slapping his legs.

"Mr. Baker, you know our destination. Lead everyone to it and hang tight." He gave his customary hand-slap and stood up. "I'll gather up our lost guys and meet you there."

Bill hugged his knees, rocking back and forth.

Dr. Greer watched him for a beat, then wagged a thumb at Bill saying "Give him some extra encouragement. He'll be fine." With that, he stood up and disappeared back the way we'd come. I watched his light flicker over the walls and fade until it abruptly disappeared to the right. He'd found the tunnel.

"Let's move, guys," I demanded.

Bill had managed to get to his feet with David's help.

"It's not too far," I assured everyone.

David gave Bill an encouraging cuff on the arm. "Close to the gold," I heard him whisper. Bill sucked in a deep breath, releasing an unsteady, "Yeah." A weak smile crossed his face and he took another deep breath. "Yeah," he repeated with resolve.

I shot David a quick nod of approval and the four of us went forward.

The closer we got to the elevator shaft, the cooler it became. I knew we were reaching the deepest part of the mine, beyond which lay the point of collapse, our ultimate destination.

Our collective lights fell on the crooked elevator in unison and we all stopped to stare at the grotesque yet strangely beautiful ruin. A visual remnant of a forgotten tragedy composed of twisted iron and a forlorn silence so deep and permanent, it was dizzying to experience. The area was like a work of art. David raised his face, his eyes bright as if he were beholding something sacred. Even though I had seen this area before, remembering it as a place of unease and violence, now it seemed oddly calm. Checko filled my thoughts and my eyes began to water as I thought of the old man. He had come to me at this very spot the last time I was here. But he had survived beyond what he experienced in this place where so many others had not. Why then, had I seen him, *talked to him* standing next to this petrified and abandoned smashed elevator cage?

Bill interrupted my musings with a drawn-out "wow" as he stared at the sight. Like David, awestruck. Beside me, Casey was frozen in a similar fashion, her mouth hanging open as she took in the surroundings. It wasn't that time stood still, so much as time ceased to exist. It could have been just getting dark above ground, or it could have been midnight. Either way, it no longer mattered. I couldn't say if I felt more alive than ever or suddenly dead. I was covered with dirt, yet I felt clean. I was in possibly the most frightening place on Earth, yet I had no fear. I was numb.

My voice came out in a monotone, indifferent. "This is where they tried to get everyone out."

"But the cable was weak."

"The cable—" David started.

"What?"

Casey grabbed my arm and pulled me to one side.

"You said, *'The cable was weak'* —" he stopped when he saw Casey pointing toward him and Bill.

"I didn't say anything," I replied, looking to where Casey pointed.

We all saw it at the same time. Me and Casey and David…and Bill, who had the best view of all.

"There was nothing to do. Nothing was left of me," the voice rasped.

"Bill…" one of us gasped.

The Play-Doh head, mishapen and white, looking out from black, button-like eyes…"Mull-dooon," it groaned…was sitting on Bill Purcell's shoulder.

We all screamed at the same time, but Bill Purcell, slowly turning his head to face the disembodied blob perched on his shoulder like an unwelcome spider, shrieked louder than everyone. The Play-Doh head turned to Bill, looking him in the eyes and responding with a tortured howl.

Bill exploded into a St. Vitus Dance, slapping his body and spinning around, his high-pitched shrieks shattering the air. He dug his feet into the ground and bolted away from us, running as fast as he could until the blackness swallowed him.

I grabbed onto David's hand, Casey grabbed onto my other hand and we ran forward, leaving the elevator behind us.

Whatever Casey and David were thinking at that moment, I didn't care. All I knew was that we had to reach the site of the collapse and was glad they were running alongside me.

———————

"Here it is."

Abandoned tools lay scattered next to the opening.

The opening itself looked bigger than I remembered; a single ledge of undisturbed stones from the collapse, easy enough to step over, lined the floor. The top was over six feet high. It looked like a doorway gone askew.

David Sills gripped his pocket Bible in both hands, eyeing me with newfound suspicion. "That thing. It took Bill."

"It was Lawrence Muldoon—" I tried to explain. "—what was left of him. It didn't mean us any harm. Bill just freaked out." My last pronouncement sounded rightfully stupid as it left my lips. Naturally, Bill was freaked out. Who the hell wouldn't have been?

Casey spoke up, coming to my defense. "Julian's right. He saw that pudgy little head weeks ago in the backyard of his aunt and uncle's. I was with Cami and Evie; he was spending the night with Rayven. It was a slumber party."

David squeezed the Bible in his hands, twisting it back and forth. "Rayven spent the night with me once."

Nodding, I said, "I know."

"It sucked," said David. "I was *so* embarrassed."

"He told me about it," I said, adding, "but that was a long time ago, Dave."

"Rayven wanted to stay up late. He wanted to watch the monster movie. I did, too. I was excited that he was spending the night."

"I know, Dave."

He wrenched the pocket Bible tighter in his fingers. "But my parents…" he growled. "So many stupid rules…*speaking in tongues.* What's that all about? *Shabba Lalla Richifara*—be in bed by seven 'o clock—*it's normalized mental illness*—" He pressed the Bible to his forehead so hard his knuckles turned white. "And at what cost? At the cost of one's family, that's what. How could my parents put me and my brothers and sisters through all this? I'm so ashamed. I wish I'd been born dead."

"You mean not born at all," Casey corrected.

160

David squeezed his eyes shut. His whole body was shaking. *"No*! I mean *born*! *Dead*! Not *never had been born*, not stillborn, but coming into life and staying a second after my first and last breath *Thank you, no.* and having an end to it."

"I would have missed you," Casey said. "I wouldn't want that for you."

"C'mon, Dave," I tried, not knowing what to say.

He gathered himself and sighed.

"We're dead," he declared. "We're all dead. Bill's dead. Rayven and Roger and Mr. Greer, they're all dead and waiting for us." With a sudden motion, he flung the Bible violently toward the dark hole. It came so close, I thought it would hit me so I flinched, but it whizzed past me through the opening. Out of reflex, I turned, shining my light into the direction of the Bible's trajectory through the hole.

Inside was a space the size of a large closet. To the left was a low opening, a small tunnel. A wide circular hole stood in the middle of the floor, leading who-knows-how-much deeper than where we stood. There were no miners, huddled together in death, no evidence at all that thirty-five men had taken refuge here to make their final stand. What were we doing in this place?

"Why did you do it?" I heard David ask.

"I don't know anymore," I said, still leaning inside the opening, my wheat light trained on the hole in the center of the ground. Casey's voice called my name. I turned back to her and David.

Casey was off to one side, her back pressed against the rough wall. She was frozen in shock, hands clenched at her waist as she gasped *"Uh-uh-uh,"* over and over. Her eyes were so wide, they looked about to pop out of her head. She was staring at David. He was floating two feet off the ground, his sightless eyes rolled up white.

Two figures held him aloft, a male and female. Their profiles were turned to him, one on each side of his face as their slithering tongues lapped over his cheeks and penetrated his ears, exiting through his nostrils. Except for their faces, they had no distinct bodies, only shimmering shroud-like forms exploring him like the tentacles of an

161

octopus. The voices of each face chortled into David's ears and over the dank space.

"Your...life..."

"*It's not real!*" Casey screamed.

"*Fight it, David!*" I yelled.

"...belongs to us, our son..."

"*They're not you parents!*" I came forward a few steps, hoping to grab David, when all Hell broke loose.

From behind me, a blue mist glowed from inside the opening, washing over the threshold and filling the area where we stood with blinding intensity. I squeezed my eyes shut, taking sightless swings in front of me. From a million miles away, I heard Casey screaming again "*Fight it, David!*" and then Casey was just screaming as I was hit by a force that knocked the air from my lungs and sent me tumbling into somersaults through the air. Balling myself up to brace against the impact, I hit the rock wall as mocking voices rattled inside my head—

"*It...*"

"*...is...*"

"*...real....*"

—before everything went black.

———————

"Come back."

Soft fingertips caressed my face, running over my temples and down my cheeks. Lips closed over my mouth, renewing me with the warmth of foreign breath. I wanted to raise my arms to hold the feeling as long as I could, but I was numb, unable to move. It felt like a dream.

"Come back to me, Julian."

Casey's face loomed over me, wrinkled with concern and covered in grimy black streaks of sweat and tears. She looked like an angel. *As always.*

"I'm Julian," I managed to say.

She kissed me again. "Yes, you are." I could hear the relief in her voice. She kissed me a third time, longer than before, her lips lingering against mine. I raised my right hand with a newfound sensation, cradling the back of her head, my fingers intertwined in her hair. I was in The Playhouse, at the slumber party, lying on my sleeping bag but, no. That wasn't right.

"It's just you and me, now."

My dad looked down at me. His face seemed so old and tired for such a young man. My necktie was too tight, making the inside of the shirt collar itchy. Grimacing, I tugged at the necktie as he led us through double doors into a larger room where a bunch of familiar people waited. Some were seated, some standing. Many of them were crying. At the front of the room was a large box. We walked deep into the room. Dad left me with a man and woman before he went up to the box. Next to the man and woman was someone I recognized from school. I smiled.

"Hi, Rayven."

Man am I drunk.

I turned to him. "Whaddaya mean 'things'? What kind of things?"

"It's different for everyone."

There he is.

Harlan Greer looked down at me with relief.

"I knew Vincent and John, your dad. That was a long time ago."

My eyelids fluttered, trying to focus my eyes. "*Why—?*"

"My family's not here. Remember the gravel road?"

I *did* remember that. The sense of loss was so lonely it made me want to cry. My lips quivered despite my best efforts to resist. Tears filled my eyes and overflowed into my ears. My nostrils grew moist and my throat clogged until finally, the only choice left was to surrender. Throwing my arms over my face, I cried freely with abandon, a montage of everything good and bad in my life, of every regret and hope I'd known, flashing through my mind. Snapshots running past my mind's eye like so many *Cliff Notes* bearing my name.

The rough earthen wall pressed painfully into my back. Jagged rocks and hard clumps of uneven dirt grated against my backbone and pushed into the skin under my shoulder blades.

I was sitting upright. My hard-hat was across the floor from me, the wheat-light illuminating the opposite wall.

It was deathly quiet. Afraid to move anything but my eyes, I scanned the area slowly, holding my breath and hoping my vision would adjust to the darkness beyond the wheat-light's glow. Arching forward away from the wall, I winced at the stinging pain over my back.

I was awake. For real this time. Wiping my eyes, I called Casey's name. Nothing. My aching body crawled over the ground, my outstretched arm straining to retrieve my hard-hat. Just beyond the light, I saw what appeared to be the silhouette of a person standing in the center of the tunnel. My fingers froze inches from the hard-hat. "Casey?" I tried.

The shape didn't move. Squinting into the darkness my eyes could just see the basic outline of a human form. Standing stock-still, the form seemed to be studying me.

As much as I wanted to grab the hard-hat and aim the light at the figure, I was paralyzed with fear.

"Julian," said the shape.

The hairs on my neck rose, so slowly I could hear the strands whispering to attention behind my ears.

The form floated closer.

Every fiber of my being cried out to bury my face in fear, to close my eyes, to curl up and hide. Resisting, I found the courage to grab the hard-hat. Taking it in both hands I shined its light directly at the shape.

It was Michelle Baker.

My mother.

She stood there, a young woman in her early thirties, her hands folded casually in front of her. She smiled at me.

"So grown up. Like I always imagined."

All I could get out was the word, "Mom." My hands were shaking so badly, I was barely able to put the hard hat on my head.

Illuminated in the full-on glow of my light, Mom was vibrant, her face framed by long brown hair. She was dressed in a Madonna concert t-shirt, faded blue jeans, and sandals. In life she had seen and been many things, only two of which had been John Baker's wife and my mother. Cancer had unjustly cut short her life much sooner than it should have, but that was all over now. I could see that clearly. The cancer which had taken her away was itself dead and gone. But Michelle Baker in her prime stood before me now.

I started toward her, but she stopped me with a raised hand.

"You can't, son. My beautiful boy. I'm sorry. You can't."

"Mom," I pleaded, "why not?"

"We don't know."

"Who...we? Who doesn't know?"

"Any of us. *All* of us, I guess."

She took her eyes off me for the first time, looking over the tunnel.

"The Black Diamond Mine. At first, I was surprised as you."

She reached out and touched the wall. Her hand pulled a loose rock away. She studied it for a second with a sad smile before letting it drop to the ground.

"Then I remembered and understood why I was here."

She brushed her hands clean of the dust from the rock.

"How have you been, Julian? Tell me, are you happy?"

"Yes, Mom, I'm happy." I felt the urge to laugh, so I did. "Not so much down here, you know? But yeah, ma, I'm happy most of the time."

"I understand. Being down here will pass, though, son."

She took a step closer to me.

"And your dad. How is he?"

"He's fine, Mom. Still playing. It's just the two of us."

"Still drumming. I'm glad to know that. Still doing what he always loved."

"He still loves you, Mom. He misses you every day. We both do."

"I know you do. I still love you both. Tell your dad that."

"I will, Mom."

She took another step forward. We were so close, I could feel her essence surrounding me, shielding me from the stale air and stifling darkness. She pointed behind me.

"What you're looking for is beyond the wall inside the opening. On the far side of the hole in the ground. I've been there and seen them. They didn't see me. I couldn't talk to them. That's where they were trapped. Where they still wait for help to come. Be careful of that hole. It's not right. Something is down there that wants to keep you all here."

"What do you mean, Mom?"

"I wish I knew, but I don't. I think the miners know. Get them out and they'll do the rest."

Tendrils of warmth passed over the back of my neck, across my cheek and returned to my mother's open fingertips, three feet away from me.

"My son. Hug your father for me."

The wheat light flickered and went out, leaving me in darkness. An instant later it flashed to life again.

The tunnel was empty.

"I will, Mom," I called into the emptiness. "I love you."

———————

"We got him, he's coming up!" yelled Bill Purcell.

I spun around to the opening at the sound of his voice.

"Hey! Where you going?!"

Casey appeared, hopping over the row of stones and rushing forward. We collided in a crushing hug. "Omigod, I thought you were dead! I propped you against the wall, but you wouldn't wake up and then Bill came through the tunnel in there and… Omigod, Julian!"

I held her tight, reassuring her. "I'm here. Little sore, but I'm here." Taking her head in my hands, I kissed her.

She stiffened and pulled back, eyeing me for a beat before returning the kiss. "I'm sorry," she said, adding, "no more high school bullshit," before kissing me again.

"Case—! Oh, hey, Julian," said Bill as he stood fidgeting in the opening. "A little help guys?"

We joined him inside the space. Bill's rope was tethered to a crooked support beam, stretched taught. Protruding from the hole, two hands clutched the rope. "Pull, *goddammit!*" demanded the voice of David Sills.

The three of us hoisted him out of the chasm. We collapsed together in a heap against the far wall. David's face was ghostly white. "My parents are screwed up," he gasped. "But they wouldn't have done this."

"It wasn't your parents," I said. "It's this place." I looked over at Bill. "What about you, man?"

Bill gave me a tight-lipped laugh and shrugged.

"He just came out of that tunnel," Casey motioned, "like nothing ever happened. He was *strolling*."

"Okay, okay," Bill said with raised hands. "I can explain. The turd-head freaked me out, but then he was alongside me and he seemed kinda...*friendly*, you know? The faster I ran, the more he kept up. Every time I looked over, there he was, his face sideways, staring at me. So finally, I stopped, I couldn't run anymore, and I hauled back to punch the squishy little bastard and he went backward like he was scared. Then he mumbled some horseshit, I don't know, like *Frollo Muldoon Muddermess Boy.*"

The tools left by Dr. Greer came flying through the opening; a pickaxe and two shovels clanking together in a heap just over the stone ledge. Grumbling under his breath, a man dressed in dungarees, white shirt, and vest stepped through the opening. He glared at Bill Purcell.

"Follow Muldoon to the motherless boy," he said. Dropping to his hands and knees, he scampered toward us like an insect, stopping at Bill's nose. "Am I speaking English?" he growled.

Bill was shocked speechless, so I answered instead.

"You are now, Larry," I said.

Lawrence Muldoon rose to his feet. He straightened his vest and turned his head to me.

"Well, what do you know? My late-night friend. How nice to see you again." He glanced back at Bill and flashed a toothy grin for a single second, before turning back to me. "I thought, well, no worries, this'll be over in a second. I won't even really feel it and at least I tried." He stopped long enough to emit a short chuckle before continuing. "It was the longest second of my life. Feet shattering, ankles breaking, hip bones punching out of my skin and going into my armpits, my ribcage sandwiched to pulp between collapsing steel, my eyes popping from—"

Maybe he saw our faces, twisted in various stages of disgust. Maybe he grew disgusted with his own memories. Whatever the reason, Lawrence Muldoon stopped. He inhaled deeply, blowing out a phantom breath.

"Anyway." He tugged at his vest again. "I've been floating around holes and trees and grass forever, scaring rabbits and squirrels and you, young man," he said to me. He stared at his hands, rubbing his palms back and forth. "And now, here I am." He ran his fingers through his hair, whispering the word "hair."

"Pick up those tools," Lawrence Muldoon said. "Finish what I couldn't do." Turning away, he stepped over the rock ledge and vanished into the main tunnel, his last words echoing through the dark, punctuated by the sound of cheerful laughter.

"Play-Doh head. What next?"

We did as Lawrence Muldoon instructed. I took up the pickaxe. Bill and Casey each grabbed a shovel.

"Right here," I said, swinging the pickaxe against the wall. The long blade buried itself into the wall of rocks like a knife through butter. The ceiling shuddered, raining stones and dirt. Lurching back, David caught me before I fell into the hole. We both exhaled. I repositioned myself, keeping an eye on the hole. David stood guard directly behind me. Casey and Bill were to my left in front of the side tunnel, holding their shovels at the ready. I raised the pickaxe for a second swing.

The wall began to crumble, slowly at first. Pebbles and dirt broke loose from the middle of the wall, trickling to the ground. I bashed the wall again as hard as I could. The pickaxe went deep. I lost my grip, the handle flying from my fingers as larger rocks broke free, falling inward to reveal blackened hands reaching from within, furiously digging outward. As the hole grew wider, the hands multiplied, becoming more frantic in their task. We'd reached the thirty-five dead miners after almost fifty years and they were more than ready to be freed.

A blast of foul wind burst from the opening, filled with the stench of ancient decay.

"Umm, maybe we should go now," David said from behind.

"No," I snapped back, standing my ground and keeping my eyes on the mummified hands as spidery fingers scratched against the hardscrabble edges of the widening hole. "We have to find Rayven and Gallo and Dr. Greer."

Casey hollered my name and then screamed.

"*Holy shit!*" Bill yelled, spinning around. He raised the shovel over his head. Casey fell to the ground as something from the side tunnel reached out and grabbed Bill.

Chapter Fifteen

Doom and Death

Casey scrambled away from the side tunnel toward the main opening as Bill struggled for control of the shovel with the hidden attacker. The horizontal handle pushed and pulled between the two pairs of hands until the handle connected firmly to Bill's chest. Losing his grip, Bill stumbled backwards, raising his fists.

"What the hell's the matter with you?!" hollered Rayven. He stepped into the space and dropped the shovel.

"*Oh, man,*" Bill exhaled. "You scared me half to death!"

"I should beat you the rest of the way to death." Rayven said to Bill with an impatient growl. Looking left and right, Rayven threw up his arms in frustration. "Where the hell are we?"

More rocks crumbled to the ground from the clawing hands. A few of the larger ones bounced over the dirt and fell into the hole. The hint of pale blue light flashed from deep in the opening. Rayven pointed to the blackened hands and then to the hole. "What the hell is *this?*"

"This is what we've been looking for," I said. "Where's Dr. Greer?"

"He's up ahead in the main tunnel." Rayven said, jabbing his index finger at the widening hole. "*Jesus,* are those—?"

"The miners, *yeah.*"

Rayven nodded, saying quickly, "Great! Mystery solved! Listen we've gotta get out of here, gotta get out of this mine as fast as we can go!" He shoved me and David in front of him and the five of us started to exit the space into the main tunnel when we heard a voice in the darkness in front of us.

"I brought a gun down here. *Uh-hee-hee.* It's a fine gun. My father's gun."

There came the sound of shuffling feet, labored breathing.

"'Always out to get you,' my father says. Never know when, never know where, never know who. *Uh-hee.* Be prepared. *Uh-hee-hee.* Always be prepared. Never know who. *Uh-hee-hee-hee.*"

I stepped forward. Rayven, David, Bill, and Casey gathered close behind me. I called into the main tunnel.

"*Roger?* Roger, we need to go, man."

More shuffling, getting closer.

"Oh, we're gonna go, man. *Uh-hee-hee-hee.* We're all gonna go."

The figure came forward into the slivers of light. We could all see it was Roger Gallo. At least his body.

He moved in jerking motions, one arm outstretched and pointing the gun. His eyes were black as the coal walls around us.

"'Get 'em before they get you,' that's what Daddy always said."

I took hold of Casey's arm and pulled her behind me. "Roger, c'mon, man—"

His face twitched to me; black eyes staring into mine.

"Had to keep pushing, didn't you? Had to find out. Had to invade this place. This place I've held long before there was ever any mine here, any people, any town."

The clawing hands of the miners were close to breaking through the wall. A steady stream of rocks and pebbles tumbled into the hole on the ground in front of us.

Roger jerked his head at the widening opening in the wall, his arm pivoting to shoot at the frantic clawing hands. The gunshot made the arms retreat, their progress halted as the shot rang in everyone's ears.

"That's loud," Roger said. "*Uh-hee.* Think they got the message?"

Bill Purcell peered over Rayven's shoulder. "We're leaving now," he said to Roger.

Before he could move, Roger fired another shot into the ceiling. "You think? *Hee-hee-uh-hee.*"

I took a step forward and held out my hand. "Roger, hey, what's going on?"

Roger fixed his black gaze on me once more.

"Playing dumb as usual. You motherless bastard."

"Hey, buddy, just take it easy," David Sills said. He spoke calmly, offering an open hand to Roger. "Rog. You're our friend, you know? You're not your father or anyone else. You belong to yourself. Taking care of each other. That's what we do." He urged Roger to him. "Let's get out of here, man."

Except for bowing his head, Roger Gallo didn't move.

"That's the way, Roger," David said.

"Yeah, Rog, yeah," Bill encouraged.

"Give me the gun," David continued.

"The gun," Roger mumbled. "*Hee-hee-uh-uh-hee-uh—*"

The moment he raised his head I could see that Roger Gallo was gone, replaced by whatever had held everyone, both dead and alive, captive in this place. It had fouled the soil for ages and would never retreat.

"David Sills, you Bible-banging little queer. *I'll give you the gun.*"

There was a blinding flash and an ear-splitting gunshot. A burst of warm and thick liquid spattered over my face and then pandemonium as we split away from the opening, Casey, Bill, and I going left, Rayven and David…

…*Rayven and David…*

…*Rayven.*

Rayven lay on the ground, David kneeling beside him. He'd jumped in front of the shot at the last second, taking the bullet meant for David.

Roger Gallo took one jerky twitching step forward, leveling the pistol at David's head.

"Too bad, so sad. *Hee-uh-uh-uh-uh-uh.*"

An avalanche of rocks tumbled into the hole in the ground as the miners broke free in a wave of purple, misty light. A deep blue light came out of the hole in a column of energy pulsing into the ceiling with increasing force.

David looked up at Roger Gallo's twisted, grinning face. He closed his eyes to brace for the end.

"Hey, kid!"

Gallo whirled around, aiming the pistol into the main tunnel. Professor Greer emerged at a full run, holding something in his hands.

"I said no open flames."

He sparked one of Bill Purcell's flares to life as Gallo fired wildly. Whether any of the shots hit him, I couldn't say. All I could see was Professor Harlan Greer connecting with Roger Gallo in a flying tackle. They went airborne into the blue light, disappearing down the hole.

The four of us took hold of Rayven and dragged him over the ledge and into the main tunnel, not stopping until we were far enough away to safely look back. The blue light was so strong now, it lit our way forward, buzzing like a generator. Watching our progress were the figures of several miners. One of the decayed figures stepped forward and waved before they all retreated into the pulsing light.

We scrambled out of the Black Diamond Mine in time to see an explosion of deep blue light bursting from the ground far away from us. It shot into the sky in a perfect column, rising above the treetops. The flaming shaft reached the night sky, stretching impossibly high.

We dragged Rayven to the Jeep and lifted him into the back seat. Bill was bruised and scratched. David's knees and elbows were raw and bloodied. Dried blood caked both sides of Casey's face from flying rocks and pebbles. My back was still oozing blood from crashing into the rocks in the excavated space. As sore and exhausted as we were, we were in better shape than Rayven.

As far as we could tell, he'd been shot in his right shoulder. There was so much blood, we couldn't be sure.

David and Bill sat on either side of Rayven as I hopped behind the steering wheel and started the engine. Seated next to me, Casey was shaking so badly I had to help her fasten her seat belt.

Throwing the Jeep into reverse, I backed away from Dr. Greer's Forester, turning the Jeep toward the path through the woods leading to Uncle Vincent's house. Before I could go forward, the ground began to rumble. The carriage of the Jeep swayed back and forth underneath its tires like some crazy thrill ride. The geyser of blue light expanded as the ground continued quaking around us. There was a sudden *POP* and the violent rumbling stopped. It was dead quiet. The shaft of blue light turned into a purplish-black cylinder of glowing energy and began to emit a low, eerie hum.

The cable holding the waiting handcar snapped without warning, sending the handcar plummeting down the tunnel. As if on cue, the once reliable entrance folded in on itself, leaving only settling ground as the dust cleared.

My foot stomped the gas pedal to the floor and the Jeep sped onto the path, leaving a cloud of dust behind us.

"How's Rayven?" I yelled from the corner of my mouth to the back seat. The path was narrow and surrounded by tall trees. I couldn't afford to look away for a second to risk a head-on collision with a tree. I couldn't afford to slow down to check for myself, either. I had to get to the house, to get Rayven help as fast as possible.

"He's asleep!" came the answer, followed by a correction in a different voice. "He's unconscious!" Who was saying what, David or Bill, I had no idea.

"Is he breathing?" I called back.

"I don't know!" someone answered.

The Jeep came out of woods into the backyard. We all saw it at once and I hit the brake. Every light inside the house was on, shining out from every window on all three floors.

Outside, both the house and grounds were illuminated with flashing lights. Several police cars were in the driveway and on the side lawn. A large group of people stood near the house, huddled together with several police officers. My stomach sank when I saw the digital clock on the dashboard. The glowing blue numbers displayed the time: *1:53am.* We'd been down in the mine for almost nine hours. Dr. Greer and Roger Gallo were dead. Rayven had been shot and the rest of us looked like hammered shit.

So much for the football game alibi.

"This isn't good," I said.

Beside me, Casey asked, "Is that for us?"

A couple of local news vans were parked on the street.

Nearby, I saw the blinking red lights of a waiting ambulance at the end of the driveway.

I gripped the steering wheel in both hands. "Yeah," I answered with a defeated sigh. "All of it." *We're in big trouble.*

Taking my foot off the brake pedal, I gunned the engine and raced over the back yard, honking the horn as we came to the back edge of the house. I yanked the steering wheel hard to the right. The Jeep went sideways before sliding to an abrupt stop.

The commotion turned to pandemonium. I watched as Dad and Uncle Vincent pushed through the line of police officers, running toward the Jeep. Three officers trotted behind them, their easy strides betraying a desire to avoid confrontation. Two officers took their places in line holding the rest of the crowd in place.

I saw the anxious faces of Aunt Laurie and Evie and Cami, craning their necks above the line of police in front of them. Then I saw Casey's parents. Then two other couples I recognized as David and Bill's parents.

Uncle Vincent and Dad came up to the driver's side. I didn't wait for them to speak.

"Rayven's hurt! He's been shot!"

"*We need medical!*" One of the officers yelled over his shoulder. Another officer reached between Dad and Uncle Vincent, opening my door. "Anyone else injured?"

I shook my head, looking down at the officer's upturned hand.

"Step on out, son, it's okay."

175

Numbly, I took hold of his hand and slid off the seat, expecting to be turned back around to face the vehicle and be handcuffed. Instead, the officer handed me off to my father. On the passenger side, another officer helped Casey out of the Jeep. To my surprise, he led Casey around the front of the vehicle to me, telling her to "Just hang right here, Miss, okay? Just take it easy." Her hand found mine, our fingers intertwining tightly.

Dad gripped my shoulder, looking me up and down. "Jesus, Julian, are you okay, son?"

I couldn't look him in the eye. "I'm okay, Dad."

David and Bill waited at the rear of the Jeep, watching as the paramedics pulled Rayven from the vehicle and onto a gurney.

Uncle Vincent stood behind the paramedics, wringing his hands as he watched them work.

They threw a blanket over Rayven's waist before huddling above his torso. I heard one of them declare, "In-and-out." Another one put an oxygen mask on Rayven's face. They pulled the blanket up to his neck and wheeled the gurney through the grass. David sprang forward, running past the paramedic at the front of the gurney only to crash headlong into Uncle Vincent.

Both paramedics stopped. David dropped to his knees, his hands clasped under his chin, repeating, "Thank you," over and over again like a sacred mantra. "You saved my life," he finished.

The blanket stirred and Rayven's forearm appeared. He gave David a thumbs-up and patted his clasped hands.

Behind him, Uncle Vincent gently took hold of David and guided him to one side before kneeling over his son.

"Hey, Dad. *We did it.*"

Uncle Vincent took hold of Rayven's hand. "You're gonna be okay," Uncle Vincent assured him. "Mom and I are gonna ride to the hospital with you."

"Okay, Dad," Rayven said. Uncle Vincent gave him a reassuring smile before sprinting over the yard back to Aunt Laurie and the twins. *"He's okay!"* he shouted to them.

As they started to move the gurney again, Rayven held up his hand for the paramedics to stop. He ushered me closer and I came up to him. I leaned down and put my ear to his cheek. Rayven wagged his index finger at the flashing lights in the sky. I could tell the paramedics must have given him a painkiller.

"All this," he slurred, his finger turning invisible circles in the air, "my insurance policy."

"I don't understand," I whispered.

He tried to laugh but managed only a high-pitched squeak from deep in his throat. "I told Evie what we were going to do. No football game. In case something happened."

I looked up at the police cars, the flashing lights, our waiting families. I nodded with understanding. "*Well...*" I continued to nod, "...something sure happened, didn't it? We solved a mystery." I laid my hand on his cheek. "Evie was a good insurance policy," I declared. Brushing his hair off his damp forehead, I added, "You saved David's life. You probably saved us all."

Rayven smiled weakly.

"I cover the waterfront," he said.

———————

Casey and I walked hand in hand next to Dad, Bill and David following closely behind us. Two policemen flanked us as we made our way back to the driveway. As we reached our separate families, Casey's hand and mine released their hold, our fingertips brushing together as we parted in silence.

A policeman waited behind Evie and Cami. The twins were staring wide-eyed at me. When I stopped in front of them, they stepped forward and hugged me.

Bill Purcell gestured wildly to his parents as he related his experience. Both stood in rapt attention, interjecting "oohs" and "ahhs" at all the right points in his retelling of events.

David held his mother's hand as he spoke. His mom and dad listened intently. The relieved expression on their faces was unmistakable.

Casey and her parents sat in a circle on the grass as she recounted what we'd been through. At one point, her mother looked over at me and smiled.

The absence of Roger Gallo's parents filled me with an odd sadness.

At last, my eyes met Dad. He looked shaky and exhausted, but there wasn't a hint of anger on his face.

"We're gonna stay here tonight with you guys," he said to the twins. "Tomorrow, we'll all go to the hospital to see Rayven."

Cami all but clapped, her face brightening as if it were just another sleepover.

Evie, on the other hand, said, "Thanks, Uncle John," all the while holding me in a cold stare. She wrapped me in a tight hug as a pretense to put her cheek against mine. I felt her breath as she growled into my ear, "You and my brother are *such assholes.*" She kissed my cheek and pulled back, holding me at arm's length. "I'm glad you're okay," she said loud enough for Cami and Dad to hear.

"We can fix you something to eat, Uncle John," Cami said with excitement. "You and Julian."

Dad nodded to the policeman standing with us. He turned to Cami. "Why don't you guys go on inside and figure out where me and Julian are sleeping tonight," he said casually.

I knew something was wrong and had a pretty good idea of what that something was.

Evie and Cami, none the wiser, went inside the house, leaving me with Dad and the police officer. Time to face the music.

A plainclothes officer introducing himself as Detective Wallis corralled the four of us at the back of a police cruiser before leading us into the backyard. He stopped at Dad's Jeep, frozen for a second while he looked it up and down. He peered into the cab. Then, he reached out and laid a hand on the roof, pulling it back as if the roof were red-hot. We continued through the yard and were almost at the tree line when he stopped us, saying, "Right here."

We all stared at our shoes. Beside me, Casey was trembling. Bill kicked at the grass. David stood stone-still. The detective called each of our names and lined us up in order from left to right. Julian Baker. Bill Purcell. David Sills. Casey Woodruff.

He held an open notepad at his chest, pencil in the other hand. "Besides Rayven Baker, is everyone here from this little adventure?" He glanced at the notepad. "Julian Baker."

"Here, sir," I said, looking up at him for the first time.

The man was sweating so much, the collar of his shirt was more gray than white. Had I not known better, it seemed like he'd been down in the mine with us. When he looked up at the four of us standing in line, his face was pale, wearing what I could only describe as a haunted expression. "Who else?"

"There was Professor Greer and our friend, Roger Gallo," I said before I started to cry. Bill put his arm around me.

"They're dead, Detective, sir," Bill said.

Detective Wallis scribbled on the notepad. "How do you know they're dead?"

"They were pretty far behind us," said David Sills.

"Everything started to collapse. They got trapped," Casey added.

A police officer came up behind Detective Wallis. The detective turned his back on us. I heard the officer say something about the Fire Department and emergency services and "the entrance is gone" and "total collapse." I heard Roger Gallo's name and the police officer say, "Family's not here, but we're in the process of notifying them." The officer continued, "The vehicle on-site is registered to a Harlan Greer, Professor at ISU, no other contact information." Detective Wallis nodded the entire time the officer relayed the information. He said something I couldn't hear to the officer. The officer said something like "I think so," or "If you say so," and returned across the yard to his fellow officers, our families, and the flashing lights.

Detective Wallis turned back to us. *"David Sills."* David took a step forward. "Yes, sir."

"How did your friend get shot?"

"It was confusing, sir." David's voice was steady and confident for the first time in his life. "It was dark and Roger got lost. Dr. Greer went to find him and got lost, too. We all brought stuff we thought we might need. Roger brought his father's gun." David reached into his jeans and produced his pocket Bible, holding it in front of him. "I brought my Bible."

Bill Purcell spoke up. "I brought some flares, but Dr. Greer said they'd be dangerous."

David glared at him. Bill shook his head and apologized, looking back down at his shoes. "Roger was so scared, he was firing the gun, you know, to signal us, but he was closer than he thought and accidentally shot Rayven. The mine started to collapse and we all panicked."

Bill couldn't help himself, blurting out, *"We saw monsters!"*

Casey punched him in the arm. "Shut up, Bill!"

"What the hell? *Oww.*" Bill grimaced. "We did," he mumbled.

Detective Wallis closed his notebook with a snap. As if agreeing, he said with a whisper, "It *was* pretty scary down there," before calling Casey's name.

Casey pushed Bill behind her as she stepped forward, defiant. "That's me," she said, her arms crossed over her chest.

"What kind of gun was it? Handgun? Rifle?" Detective Wallis asked the question as if he already knew the answer.

Casey stuck her chin out at him. "It was a pistol, okay?"

"Calm down, young lady," the man said. He stared past us into the tree line and beyond as if in a trance. The notebook had disappeared back into the pocket of his suit jacket. After a long pause, he motioned us to him, as close as a quarterback calling the next play. As we huddled, Detective Wallis loomed over us and said, "Don't do anything like this again, you understand? I think we're done here. Go back to your parents."

Without a word, Bill took off, speed walking across the yard. Casey followed, turning around to give me a last look. "See you," was all she said.

David and I walked together in silence until he split off to join his family. Mr. and Mrs. Sills stretched out their arms to him as David's brothers and sisters stood clustered together behind them, all wearing waif-like anxious expressions.

Up ahead, my dad waited for me, hands on his hips. I glanced over my shoulder to see Detective Wallis still at the tree line, staring up at the sky. The explosion lighting up the night above Crumpton Hill had faded. In its place was a pale bluish fog, dissipating to reveal a blanket of stars.

I was exhausted, filthy and numb. The image of Dad grew closer and closer to me, as if I were watching a film instead of moving steadily toward him under some hidden energy inside myself I could neither feel nor direct. It was only when I felt Dad pull me to him, I realized I had walked across the yard under my own steam. I clung to him like a frightened child, grateful for the warmth of his embrace, the protection I felt from his strength. I was closer to becoming an adult than ever before, but in that moment all I wanted to do was to remain the kid who could count on anyone but himself to protect him from the world.

"Mr. Baker." It was Detective Wallis. I felt dad's body shift as he shook the detective's hand. "I understand your brother's property includes the area around the mine entrance?"

"That's right," Dad said.

Detective Wallis nodded. "The damage from the explosion was contained within that property. As bad as this is, it could have been much worse." I felt the detective's hand between my shoulder blades. "Your son was very cooperative."

"Kids," Dad said. He paused. I could tell he was trying to be as nonchalant as possible. "They can do stupid things."

Suddenly, Detective Wallis' voice was close to my ear. "I'm sorry about your friends," he whispered.

"Thank you," Dad said. "If you need anything else—"

"Appreciate it," the detective said.

When I found the courage to open my eyes, Detective Wallis, along with two or three uniformed police, had moved on to the parents of Bill, David, and Casey. Before long, I watched my friends leave. One by one, the police cruisers killed the flashing lights and pulled away from the house.

Cami leaned out the front door, declaring brightly, "We got the extra bedroom on the third floor all set up!"

Dad thanked her. "Everyone's gone now, sweetheart. You and your sister can go on to bed. We'll be up in a minute."

"Gotcha, Uncle, *goodnight!*" Cami said, pulling the door closed. The sound of her footsteps over the hardwood floor inside the foyer turned to fading stomps as she climbed the stairs to her bedroom.

"Goddamn third floor," Dad said, doing the *under-his-breath* thing. "Living room couch would have been fine." He caught me shaking my head. "*Guilty,*" he confessed. "Old habits die hard." He looked me up and down, wrinkling his nose at my blackened face, the blotches of dried blood scabbed across my cheeks and shirt.

"You need a long hot shower. I'll grab some clothes from Rayven's room and make us a couple sandwiches in the meantime."

That sounded so good. To wash myself clean, fill my rumbling stomach, and collapse into sleep. Instead, I asked Dad if we could sit for a while longer.

We went around the house and took up two seats on the back deck, staring over the yard into the woods beyond.

Inside my spinning head, an image flashed of Dr. Greer's Subaru Forester left waiting at the mine entrance for an owner who would never return to claim the vehicle. That image was followed by all of us clustered together in the high school cafeteria, Rayven throwing French fries across the table into Roger Gallo's open mouth while David and Bill cheered them on. After that, the Immigrant Fountain and Casey Woodruff's eyes looking deep into mine. "Did you win?"

"I pledge allegiance."

"No, you're *not* in luck!" Mrs. Stringfellow's face.

"Uncle John's never told you." Rayven's face.

Uncle Vincent's face. "Things DO come out at night."

"No open flames." Dr. Greer.

"Motherless bastard." Roger Gallo.

"We're your friends." David Sills.

So many faces and moments and words spoken and paths taken and paths undiscovered and decisions made and brief tender connections and endless longings and sudden conflicts and fates sealed and profound confusion and absolute certainly and fear and confidence and all of it real, the visions and ghosts and intuitions and my father and mother and friends all coalescing into an electric-blue narrow funnel piercing dead-center into my chest, invading the vessel of my body to become memories, the good and the bad and the mundane, flooding my senses and filling me up to leave me reeling.

I felt the wooden Adirondack chair against my back. My mental onslaught subsided, leaving a final declaration tingling inside me:

I am Julian Baker and that's enough.

Sitting next to me, Dad lit a cigarette and blew a cloud of smoke into the night air. We had sat down only a heartbeat ago.

"*Finally,*" Dad whispered. He took a couple more drags before flicking the cigarette off the deck. "It's so nice out here." He shivered and squared his shoulders before settling back in the chair. "Little chilly, though."

"Uh-huh," I replied.

Dad crossed his legs and folded his hands over his chest.

"Didn't know your friend Roger very well. I remember meeting him once. Seemed like a good kid, bud. I'm sorry."

My lips quivered. *From the cold,* I told myself. "Me, too. He had some problems," I managed to say.

"Don't we all," Dad replied. I heard him whisper "Harlan" and closed my eyes. It was all I could do not to break down.

"We knew each other, you know," he continued in a voice so casual; I was taken aback. "Long time ago. He wanted to buy this property, but your uncle didn't want to sell. I finally warned him to leave Vincent alone."

"Or piss blood," I said.

Dad laughed. "Told you that, did he? Harlan knew what was going on out here. Maybe even before we did. He was only trying to help Vincent and Laurie, I think. He was a good guy. I'm glad the two of you met."

I pitched forward and caught my head in both hands, pressing back sobs.

"Hey, hey, now," Dad said softly in my ear. His hand rubbed my back as he continued to speak. "Harlan was no fool, son. Whatever he needed to do, he knew it wouldn't be easy. He knew he needed you to help him get it done. C'mon. Look out there."

I raised my head to the dark yard. There was nothing to see. No grotesque monsters or animated phantoms dancing over the grass. There never would be again.

"It was no accident the two of you met. I think I believe there are no accidents." Dad stood up reaching into his breast pocket as he pivoted in front of me. "Grabbed this shirt out of the closet before coming up here after Vincent called to tell me Evie had snitched you guys out. Haven't worn it in a long time." His hand came out of the pocket holding two strips of paper.

"I swore I'd lost these years ago. It was our first date."

In his palm were two wrinkled and faded ticket stubs to a Madonna concert.

"These belong to you now. I think your mom would like that." A single tear rolled down his cheek. "She loved you more than anything, son."

I took the ticket stubs gently from his hand and stood up, trying to find the right words. "Dad. I *saw*—" I stopped as I looked at him. His face was so peaceful it was almost glowing.

He nodded and said, "No accidents."

We embraced, hugging more tightly than we ever had or ever would again. "Thank you, Dad."

Something caught my eye far across the yard. Three figures standing at the tree line, studying us. The man and woman were holding hands. On the other side of the man, a child clung to his leg.

Harlan Greer and his family.

A heavy breeze blew over the treetops. I raised my chin from Dad's shoulder to look up at the rustling leaves.

When I looked down again, they were gone.

PART THREE

The Whole Wide World

Chapter Sixteen

Saying Goodbye

A little over two years after that night, Uncle Vincent and Aunt Laurie divorced. Although nothing more than chirping crickets and croaking frogs ever came out at night again at the house, their problems had been larger than nighttime phantoms and were theirs alone. Vincent and Laurie solved them as best as they knew how. Aunt Laurie bought a cozy house in Rosedale but remained close to Vincent. Neither one of them ever remarried, remaining single for the rest of their lives.

Rayven, Evie, and Cami had moved away by then, attending three different colleges. Still, the divorce came as a shock to everyone and they dealt with it in their own, very different ways. Cami took it the hardest, forever conflicted about how best to share her time between her mom and dad. She graduated from nursing school and married an anesthesiologist. They live in Chicago and have three kids. They visit when they can, which isn't often.

Evie—*Eve* nowadays—became an Assistant District Attorney in Kansas City. A confirmed bachelorette, she lives in a large condo in the trendy Power and Light District of the city with a Rottweiler named Judge. She has not returned to Harris since her parents' divorce.

Rayven never mentioned Roger Gallo's name in his statement to the police, further claiming all he remembered was being knocked unconsciousness by a falling rock. He went on to earn his bachelor's degree in English, with a minor in Political Science.

Frustrated with the perceived limitations higher learning placed on him, Rayven became a Forest Ranger, working in various national parks across the Southwest until finally landing in Colorado. He became a Hotshot, one of an elite group battling wildfires across the Southwestern forests. We talk on the phone once every couple of weeks or so. He tells me about the Rocky Mountains and all the beauty he's seen in the high country, downplaying the danger he faces on the job. I regale him with stories about the same old places and how nothing much has changed. He calls me his anchor. He's retained all his charm of our high school days, still upbeat and easy to laugh, ever boisterous and protective of the underdog. Even though he goes out on the occasional date, he always falls back on the demands of his job as the reason for never settling down. The truth is being a free spirit agreed with him. He was at peace and content with life.

When his calls caught me on a bad day to find me bitching about this or that, mostly minor, unimportant things, I could always count on him to pull me out of my funk.

"I'm sorry to hear that, Jules. A flat tire, huh? That's *rough.* All I did last week was spend fifteen hours digging a firebreak and then hiking out five miles to the nearest road. But a *flat tire?!* I don't know how you do it, man! I'll bet you had to wait, what? Fifteen, twenty minutes for the tow truck? And then for someone to fix it, what? Half-hour? And garages always have shitty magazines in their waiting area."

Bill Purcell owns a service station in Harris and is considered the best mechanic in town. I see him every few months when I bring our cars in for maintenance. We make small talk and laugh a lot, neither of us ever mentioning our night in the Black Diamond Mine.

David Sills graduated from UC San Diego with a master's degree in computer science and lives in West Hollywood, California.

On the evening of our high school graduation, seven months after we'd solved the mystery of the Black Diamond Mine, our little group remained inseparable. After the pomp-and-circumstance of the formal ceremony, everyone filtered out of the high school. Eventually, we converged behind Pastore Lumber. It was the last time we'd all be together.

Rayven, David, and Bill were already there, seated on pallets and enjoying their beers, when Casey and I joined them.

"No Juniors allowed!" the three shouted at Casey.

She flipped them the bird with a smile. "I'm not a Junior anymore!"

"She's right!" Rayven cheered making kissing noises at the two of us. "She's one of us by proxy!"

The three of them burst into loopy laughter.

Casey let go of my hand, marching up to them. She put a finger to her lips and looked up at the sky. "I know you guys from somewhere," she mused, pointing her finger at each in turn.

"Fell into a hole," she said to David.

"Can't remember anything," she said to Rayven.

"Failed prospector," she said to Bill.

Snapping her fingers, she exclaimed "I got it! *Tunnel rats!*"

Casey took a bow. Everyone applauded.

Less than an hour later, our party was in full swing. David was deconstructing religion to Bill, who listened with mouth agape, nodding in between swigs of beer. Rayven and I regaled Casey with how we'd hit that double cheese and salami win before we'd run into her at the Immigrant Fountain months earlier and a lifetime ago.

A red Impala sped into the back lot, crashing the party as it crunched to a stop in the gravel.

Jeff Lentz, a fellow graduate, stuck his head out of the driver's side, wearing an animated expression. *"Roger's old man just got killed on the Interstate!"* With that, the Impala sped away, leaving us dumbstruck. Presumably, Jeff felt it his duty to act as impromptu Town Crier and was off to spread the grisly news to others as fast as he could.

Dan Gallo was killed in a single-car accident on Interstate 70. Drunk out of his mind, the police later estimated his speed at 91 miles per hour when his car collided with a concrete construction barrier.

Shortly following her husband's death, Irene Gallo left Harris for parts unknown. Neither of them ever acknowledged the death of their son publicly—or privately from what I've heard folks in Harris say in hushed whispers.

I think about Roger Gallo frequently; about the kid he was and the adult he might have become. For many years, I was left with a nagging frustration and deep longing for answers.

But some mysteries can never be solved.

I've made peace with that fact.

———————

Casey and I became an official couple as she entered her senior year in high school. I was starting my freshman year at Indiana State University in Terre Haute. It was the best of all possible worlds. I could continue the status quo by staying at the house with Dad and continuing my relationship with Casey.

My life was perfect. The future stretched before me, promising to be bright, filled with smooth-sailing and the fulfillment of whatever dream I chose to pursue.

Despite our finest blueprints, time is an impatient arbiter of the human journey. Time never so much as takes a pause, forever moving forward in pursuit of a destination known only to itself.

Casey and I remained together throughout the next year.

After graduating high school, she enrolled at ISU. While I struggled to figure out a major, Casey planned from the start to get a teaching degree. We grew closer than ever during that year, but our time together would come to a bittersweet end as our college plans moved in different directions. She remained in touch with me and her best friends, Cami and Evie.

———————

Two years after leaving ISU, I earned my Bachelor' Degree in behavioral psychology at Indiana University in Bloomington. After four more years at the University of Michigan at Ann Arbor, I was finally done with the halls of academia. It was time to take a rest. And so, as newly minted psychologist Dr. Julian Baker, the ink still drying on my Ph.D., I returned to the familiar surroundings of Harris, to home and Dad.

John Baker had grown old. Although he was still the same person who'd raised me as a widowed father, exposing me to his free-wheeling lifestyle as a working musician, expertly balancing his role as parent and friend, the visible change was startling. His once-long brown hair was now short and grey and thinning. He moved slower than I'd remembered, leading with stooped shoulders and taking deliberate steps, instead of the usual bouncing gait I'd always known. After only seven years!

A few weeks after I'd settled in back home, we were sitting in the living room watching the late-night monster movie when my mind stumbled headlong into the answer. After high school, I saw Dad less and less, even during the first two years at ISU when I still lived at home. But after that, we saw each other during brief visits home six times a year, then three times, then twice each year. When I came home after earning my Ph.D., we hadn't seen each other for almost two years. My image of him had frozen in my mind shortly before I turned twenty. Now, I was almost twenty-eight years old and Dad was in his mid-sixties.

For father and son, seven years was a lifetime.

I began working for the county health department a few months later, in an entry-level position. Salary and Status was of little consequence to me; I was just tired of sitting around. Nevertheless, the position paid well for a new employee his co-workers addressed as "Doctor." It took me a long time to get over my discomfort at the title.

One Saturday afternoon I was at the IGA doing the weekly grocery shopping when John Baker died of a heart attack. I found him in his favorite chair as I returned from the store. He looked like he was sleeping. He had a smile on his face.

Dad was gone.

Scott Watson and Jack Cascio came together with me, Uncle Vincent, and Aunt Laurie to help with Dad's funeral. Finny Philchek had succumbed to cancer years before, when I had been a graduate student working on my master's thesis. Scott and Jack had been family to Dad as much as anyone and both were devastated when he passed. Although The Strays hadn't performed in public for many years, they still got together and jammed once a week, vowing to play to the last man. Scott and Jack would be gone a year later, both passing away in the same month.

Jack manned the guest book, standing behind a narrow podium and greeting incoming mourners with proper solemnity. Scott hosted a side room where people could retreat into an informal atmosphere after paying their respects in the larger room containing Dad's open casket. The side room turned into a boisterous affair filled with both sobbing and raucous laughter as Dad's friends shared their memories. The heavy dank odor of marijuana wafted from the room. It became so strong that one could smell it as they opened the entrance door to the funeral home. When the funeral home director pulled Scott aside to complain, Scott told him to fuck off. Undaunted, the director came up to me as I stood next to the casket. The funeral director began to admonish me about the crowd in the side room.

Uncle Vincent rose from his chair in the front row and came up to us. Without a word, he closed one hand over the back of the man's neck and steered him out of the room.

No one saw the funeral director for the rest of the service.

Later, Uncle Vincent recounted the incident: "After we got out into the foyer, I told him if he bothered the family again, he'd be spending the fifteen thousand dollars we'd paid him to celebrate my brother's life on his own goddamn funeral."

I spent the next few hours standing at the head of Dad's casket, accepting condolences from strangers and a few familiar faces from my high-school days whose names I struggled to remember. Bill Purcell

194

came up to me, holding back tears as we embraced. "Man, oh, man," was all he managed to say before we embraced. He hadn't needed to say anything, though. His presence was enough.

Flower arrangements from absent mourners surrounded each end of the casket. Rayven had sent a huge living wreath. Evie and Cami had each sent elaborate arrangements. But one particular memorial stood out.

A full-sized floral drum set with *John Baker* spelled out over the cloth bass drumhead in delicately placed rose petals.

As the service concluded and the casket was closed for transport, I finally had a chance to take a closer look at the elaborate offering. A small card hung from a branch fashioned like a cymbal stand.

Thinking of you during your loss. Always. David Sills.

The long day ended with the burial service at Roselawn Cemetery on the outskirts of Harris. Uncle Vincent, Scott Watson, Jack Cascio, and I were the pallbearers. Our heads bowed; we carried Dad the short distance from the hearse across manicured grass to his appointed final resting place.

After the gravesite service, the mourners rose and filtered over the grass to waiting vehicles under the clear afternoon sky. Aunt Laurie gave me a hug. "Come and see me, Julian. I'm always here for you," she said. Uncle Vincent stood behind me. Laurie sidestepped me to give Vincent an awkward hug. She brushed her hand over his cheek and turned away. We both watched her walk to her car and drive out of the cemetery.

Uncle Vincent glanced back at the line of chairs under the temporary awning in front of the open gravesite. "It was good. A good service."

"A long day," I added, staring off into the distance at our two remaining cars.

"Anything you need?" asked Uncle Vincent.

I shook my head.

We walked together side-by-side between the gravestones. Before splitting off to our separate cars, Uncle Vincent revealed one final secret.

The next day was Saturday. I was haunting the lonely house with nothing in particular to do when there was a knock at the door. It was Casey Woodruff.

Chapter Seventeen
Falling Like Rain

Twenty years have passed since that night in the Black Diamond Coal mine. Some mornings when I look into the mirror with a thirty-seven-year-old face, I see a reflection of the seventeen-year-old kid I used to be. We smile between the glass at each other, separated by time but still friends.

I sold the house Dad and I shared shortly after Uncle Vincent died. The secret he'd shared at Dad's funeral had come full circle at the reading of his will. Rayven and his sisters were well provided for financially. To their credit, they were the same people I'd known and grown up with. They were not greedy or in any way indignant, having forged their own fulfilled lives. They were only happy for me when I inherited Uncle Vincent's house. Included with the deed and other pertinent papers was the following letter in Uncle Vincent's handwriting:

Dear Nephew,

Although you knew this would come to be someday, as you read this, that day is here. Your cousins will not be surprised as this was a conversation we had some years ago. Although we were no longer together at the time, I included your Aunt Laurie in the discussion as well. She is still part of the family and I hope you will remain close. I know she wants that as well.

Everyone agreed that you should have the house after I passed. If you're reading this, I obviously have died, but don't worry about that. I am certainly not worried about anything now.

As you know, it is a fine house, grand in its way. You spent a lot of time here growing up, at least during the daytime. Because of you, my children had many good memories to keep them going in their early years. They think of you as their own brother, especially Rayven.

And because of you, nights up there became less...how can I put this...active.

So, you deserve the house. You've earned it.

That said, I put no "dying wishes" or stipulations on what now belongs to you and you alone.

You are free to sell the property and do as you choose with all proceeds. You are free to rent the house, donate or bulldoze it over, whatever you please.

You are also free to live in the house, to make it your own and fill it with your own memories. There are many avenues to take.

Those choices are yours now, Julian. May your life be filled with love and adventure until you reach your journey's end.

I wish you every happiness along the way.
Vincent Francis Baker

It can be frightening, this vast sprawling mansion with three floors sitting in the middle of nowhere on top of Crumpton Hill. There are rooms I haven't been inside for months. At night, the place looks like a haunted mansion from the outside. Shadows flicker and dance under the stately gables and shimmer over the yard. But there are no phantoms here, any longer. Only the wind and one's imagination.

I have a small private practice out of my office in Terre Haute close to the ISU campus, specializing in working with children. In addition, I work with local hospitals and as a consultant for the State Health Department. It's a comfortable living and I enjoy the work.

When Casey showed up at my doorstep, it was like we'd never been apart. After earning her Doctorate in Education, she traveled the country, from the coast of Maine to the Grand Canyon. She was in

Chicago visiting Cami when she heard about Dad. The next day she drove to Harris. After not seeing each other for years, we took up as if it had been yesterday.

We were married eight years ago at the Presbyterian Church in Harris. Rayven flew in from Colorado to be my Best Man. Cami and her family made the trip from Chicago. Evie came in from Kansas City. They were Casey's Maids of Honor. Cami's two daughters were the flower girls and her son was the ring bearer. After a beautiful ceremony, the reception went on long into the night.

Casey is a Professor of Social Science at ISU. During the week, we often have lunch together, schedules permitting.

Recently we've been thinking of how best to scale back our work commitments. At the end of July our twin boys, Vince and John, will start first grade and we want to have as much time to spend with them as possible. Even though we have campouts in The Playhouse during the weekends, Casey and I sitting at the entrance of the Quonset hut while the boys scramble over the yard in the dark chasing lightning bugs, we want more time with them now as they get older. I'd like to take them through the woods to the pond more often, teach them how to fish, which really isn't about fishing at all, but about patience and quiet appreciation for nature and family.

I visit the pond on a pretty regular basis myself, after solitary walks through the woods. Sometimes I bring a pole and do a little fishing. Mostly I just move amongst the trees letting the sunlight warm me until I reach the edge of the water to lie down in the long blades of grass.

It is my time machine, this place.

I can hear Rayven, his excited shouts as we caught enough fish for the slumber party fish-fry. I can hear his expressions of fear, too, about his future and the future of his mom and dad. I remember us running from this place, afraid we wouldn't make it back before nightfall. Looking across the shimmering water, I remember all these things with one important difference. While the memories remain clear and strong, they no longer contain the fearful urgency of the past. They are welcome fragments of my history and nothing more.

Somewhere beyond the pond, past another stand of deep woods, I can picture the entrance to the Black Diamond Coal Mine. Though it is part of our property, we've allowed the area to grow free and wild. The path has disappeared into the underbrush. Likewise, I imagine all above-ground evidence of the mine itself is gone. Since that final frantic flight through the woods with my friends, I've never gone back there or even been curious as to what the site looks like today. As far as I know, Dr. Greer's Forester remains there even now, a ruined shell swallowed up by time and untamed growth.

———————

Shortly before Labor Day weekend on a warm and sunny afternoon a few years ago, Vince and John pelted my squirming body mercilessly with a flurry of Nerf darts, giggling insanely as I pretended to die. Rolling and twitching, I flopped over the grass doing my best Warren Beatty from *Bonnie and Clyde.* Guns empty, the boys launched themselves with a running jump onto me. We rolled around like a single entity, growling and laughing together, coming to a stop in a tangled heap.

"Mommy!" Vince squealed with delight. Both he and John broke off their attack to cling to her legs.

I put a hand to my forehead, shielding my eyes against the sunlight.

Casey stood over us, cellphone pressed against her ear. She stared down at me as she listened to the call, her face filled with anguish. I recognized Evie's voice coming through the cell phone. *Eve,* the take-no-prisoners Assistant District Attorney was sobbing hysterically, screaming her brother's name.

———————

bulletin...United States Forest Service (USFS)...three members of the IHC...<interagency hotshot crew>...confirmed dead after their escape route was cut-off due to high winds exacerbating the fast-moving Gold Camp Canyon Fire west of Colorado Springs, Colorado. Officials report that the 6,000-acre wildfire is 3% contained. The bodies of the hotshots have not yet been recovered and their identities are being withheld pending notification of family members.

———————

As far as the universe was concerned, everything was in its place. Time chugged along unabated. But to say the universe and time exist without meaning is an easy mistake of omission we all make.

Meaning completes the trinity of universe and time.

Rayven and his twin sisters grew up together and shared many of the same experiences. He loved them both equally and they loved him equally as well. These statements are true.

Cami looked up to her older brother and loved him unconditionally. This is also true. But a more complicated truth existed between Rayven and his other sister.

Evie was often at loggerheads with Rayven, even into adulthood. She refused to put up with his nonsense if she felt Rayven had gone too far. In my mind's eye, I can remember the first night I spent at Uncle Vincent's house, I can see the rage on Evie's face after Rayven had called her friend, Casey, a *chickenshit*. In that moment Evie looked capable of murdering her brother. While Cami and Casey stood by, Evie called him an asshole. Yet, not long after, Rayven had lied to everyone except Evie about our plans to conquer the mystery of why horrible things came out at night at their home. Evie had known the truth for hours before telling anyone where we were. What had Rayven called her that night as he was led away on the gurney?

In case something happened...my insurance policy.

When he became a Hotshot, hers was the only name and number he had provided to his employer to notify "in case of emergency."

To the world, including those closest to them, they interacted like oil and water. But they both shared an unshakeable trust between them, knowing they could count on the other in a clutch, no matter the situation. When she received the call from the US Forest Service notifying her of Rayven's death, Evie allowed herself a couple of minutes to absorb the devastating news while sitting alone in her office. Then, she picked up the phone to honor the covenant between her and her brother for one final time. She called me.

———————

We hosted a formal memorial for Rayven at our house on the last Friday in August, the first day of the Little Italy Festival.

The kitchen was filled with food and drink served buffet-style. Casey opened every window in the house from the first floor to the third floor to allow the cool late-summer breezes to freshen the rooms.

Sensing something special in the air, Vince and John ran around like little savages through every room and every floor, stomping up the stairs and down again to rush through the living room into the kitchen, providing a welcome distraction for the gathering. The night before we'd explained to them how their uncle was gone and we were going to have a party for everyone who knew him. Casey said that Uncle Rayven had been in an accident so he wouldn't be able to come to the party. This news made them sad. We told them it was okay to be sad for a little while, but even though Uncle Rayven wouldn't be here, he was very happy that we were having a nice party for him.

John had an epiphany. "We have to take pictures to send him!"

"Pictures!" Vince echoed. "So he can remember it forever!"

Casey drew the boys to her. "That's a great idea. He'll love that," she assured them. "Now, why don't you go to your rooms and make sure everything looks good."

We listened to the boys gallop up the stairs into their bedrooms. Casey exhaled, swatting her hair from her forehead. She caught me staring at her. "I know. I'm a mess."

I took her arm in my hand, turning it slightly to reveal a faded discoloration the size of a pinhead.

I kissed the graphite-colored dot. "You're perfect, my love."

"Here's to Johhny West, fastest gun in the backyard," she said with a hint of sadness in her smile.

I kissed her arm again. "To Johnny West," I echoed. "Resting in peace in some Indiana landfill."

Casey laughed. "In *pieces.*"

"Yep," I said, managing to chuckle before hearing myself say "That was something else. Kinda miss him."

Casey put her arms around my neck and laid her head on my chest. "Me, too."

Aunt Laurie was the first to arrive. We took her into the library off the living room to console her. She was holding up well but I could see the lingering shock in her glazed, tired eyes. We shared memories of Rayven in between tears.

Casey's parents, Michael and Jean Woodruff, joined us a while later.

Cami and her family arrived next. The house became more active as more people arrived, helping to lighten the mood, dispersing the pall of gloom inside the house.

Aunt Laurie embraced Cami, fawning over her three grandchildren. Casey led Cami and her family up to the room we'd prepared for them.

David Sills arrived with Chris, his husband. I embraced them both on the doorstep, ushering them inside. We went upstairs, to the third floor, where I opened a door into a bedroom David remembered.

"Make yourselves comfortable," I said. To David: "My dear friend."

"Rayven's old room," he said, fighting back tears.

Other people arrived throughout the day to pass through and pay their respects; acquaintances from high school, a few of Casey's colleagues from ISU, and several of Aunt Laurie and Uncle Vincent's friends. As the day went on, Casey and I saw little of each other. She did the lion's share of juggling our boys and Cami's kids in addition to playing hostess to everyone while I brought up the rear as host, trying to give equal attention to everyone as best as I could. The kids finally found their way to The Playhouse in the yard.

I was sitting in the library catching a little break when I heard someone call my name. Rising from my chair, I peeked around the threshold to the foyer.

The front door was open wide.

Eve, dressed in a dark-blue business skirt and white tailored blouse stood in the doorway holding a single bag. Her face was red and puffy, her eyes dark slits. Her jaw was so tight in her effort to stem the tide of emotion, it looked like she had no mouth at all. For a second, I barely recognized her. The pain inside her had become visible. I could feel it flowing into me as I came up to her. All I could do was whisper her name. Eve was unable to make a sound as we searched each other's eyes.

Coming up the sidewalk behind her was Bill Purcell. It was obvious Bill had just enough time to change into a clean pair of jeans before coming over. He still wore the grease-streaked light blue shirt he sported every day at his garage. I could see the embroidered patch bearing the name *Bill* over his breast pocket. Recognizing Eve, he quickened his step as he called her name. Reaching us, he leaned down toward Eve's bag. "Let me help you with that." His fingers brushed over the handle and her closed hand. Before he could take it, she let the bag drop to the sidewalk.

Without warning, Eve exploded.

Whirling around, she crouched and raised clenched fists at Bill.

"Back off me, *goddamn you!*"

Bill flinched, going pale and taking a step back. The poor guy had no idea what was happening. He backpedaled away from Eve before stopping halfway down the sidewalk.

"Evie, I'm sorry," he called to her. "I was just trying to help you." He looked down at his shoes. "It's nice to see you again," he mumbled.

Eve turned to me. Her face was flushed. All I could do was give her a sad smile. She was fighting with every ounce of her strength to hold herself together and losing fast. She collapsed into my arms, sobbing.

Bill was frozen, still having no idea what to do. He raised his hands as if surrendering to a Swat Team.

"Julian. I'm sorry, man. I'm gonna go."

Eve clung to me, her body shaking so hard, I had to shuffle my feet to keep my balance.

I shook my head and mouthed "It's okay," to Bill. "Come on up."

Eve wailed into my chest, sobbing Rayven's name and apologizing to everyone and no one; to me and Bill, to Rayven, to herself. In her quest to achieve a place in the world, she had hidden all her vulnerabilities and pain behind a vast psychic dam of her own construction for a long time. Neither an ideal strategy nor a trait unique to her alone, but rather the same dam all of us build to varying degrees with differing outcomes. For Eve, her dam had finally burst in that moment on the doorstep, emptying so much pain from inside her to dissipate into the open spaces of the outside world. I could almost see the ethereal flood of her angst flowing out from that dam to make room for the fresh waters of healing.

"*Oh, Julian,*" she cried into my shirt. "*Oh, Goddamnit, Julian! Goddamn it! Goddamn it!*"

As she clung to me. I held her tight, whispering the name only friends from her long-ago past knew her by.

"I know. I know, *Evie,* I know. It's okay. You're home now."

Returning up the sidewalk to us, Bill leaned down to grab Eve's bag and stopped. His hand hovered with uncertainty above the leather handle. Sensing him behind her, Eve raised her head from my chest and turned to him. "Billy, I'm so sorry."

Before Bill could take up Eve's bag, she let go of me to hug him.

From inside the house, I heard Casey calling Evie's name. Eve went past me and Bill to embrace her best friend. Bill and I stepped inside the house and I closed the door behind us.

Casey said to Eve in a familiar conspiratorial whisper, "I've got you set up in your old room." She took Eve's bag from Bill and the two of them climbed the stairs.

After Casey and Eve had gone, Bill was still a little shaky. Wringing his hands, he exhaled with a nervous chuckle.

Nudging him in the ribs, I said, "Let's get a beer."

He slapped my arm. "Yeah, *Jesus.* A beer. Maybe a couple of 'em."

We went into the kitchen. I handed him a bottle of Miller Lite from the cooler sitting on the kitchen island. He twisted off the cap and took a quick pull, swallowing hard. "That's good. Super-cold." He took a second, longer swallow. "Remember that beer we all used to drink? What the hell was it called?"

"Falstaff," I answered. "They don't make that one anymore."

———————

We found ourselves alone in the kitchen, enjoying the quiet which had fallen over the house.

"…he *told* me there was gold down there…!"

I took a drink from my beer, almost choking mid-swallow as I laughed. "Did you really believe him?"

Bill cracked open a fresh can and took a drink. "Hell, I *still* believe him!" He set the beer on the counter next to the sink. "Hey," he said. "Remember seventh grade? When Rayven tried to ask that girl out?"

"Janice Harvey," I said.

"Yeah, Janice Harvey! He went up to her and—" Bill pressed a fist to his mouth. I could see he didn't know whether to laugh or cry. "—acted like he was a Knight—" Struggling to contain his laughter, Bill's face turned red. "And he said, 'May I have a date with M' Lady?'"

"And then he curtsied," I said.

Bill laughed into his fist, tears streaming down his eyes as he nodded.

"…and the girl slammed her book bag down on the back of his head!" I said.

We both exploded with laughter.

Bill wiped his eyes, composing himself. "Oh, God, was that funny! What ever happened to her?"

"Dunno." I said, suddenly sober. "Moved away, I guess."

"Yeah. Janice Harvey." Bill threw his head back and drained the beer, tossing the empty can into the sink.

Casey appeared at the kitchen door. "Julian. There's someone here."

———————

Bill was opening yet another can of beer. *"Bring 'em in!"*

Before he could take a drink, Casey came into the kitchen and took the beer from his hand. "Thank you, Bill." She took a long draw from the can. "Just what I needed." There was a bewildered look on her face.

"What's going on?" I asked.

"Rick Wallis is here."

The name didn't ring any bells. I shrugged.

"Sure," Bill said. "The retired cop. He was in for an oil change a couple weeks ago. You remember him, Jules—" Bill broke into a bad impersonation—"'*Awright, you meddling kids, line up...*'"

With a tight-lipped smile, Casey pointed at Bill.

"*Detective* Wallis," I said.

They both nodded at me.

Bill turned to the cooler to grab another beer. "He really should think about getting a new car. High-mileage oil only goes so far."

"I haven't seen him since that night, what, twenty some years ago? I mean, I've seen him around town, but..." I looked at Casey, confused.

It was her turn to shrug. "He offered me his condolences and asked to see you. He's waiting in the library."

The man had grown old, gaunt, and stooped. Standing in front of a bookshelf, hands behind his back as he studied the titles, he turned as I closed the door. His voice was feathery and faint. "Long time, no see."

I thanked him for coming and gestured to a chair. He expressed his sympathies and sat down. I sat opposite him on the other side of a large oak coffee table as casually as I could, offering him something to drink and some food, which he declined. His watery blue eyes looked over the room as he leaned forward, clasping his hands between his knees and rolling his thumbs. It occurred to me that he was as uncomfortable as I was at that moment.

"I saw the memorial announcement in the paper. I wanted to come. It seemed like the right time to come."

"Yes, sir," I said, still confused. "You're welcome here. I appreciate you stopping by."

His hands stopped fidgeting, clasped so tight I could see his knuckles turn pale. "You look good. Little bigger than I remember." He tried to smile at his attempt at levity but grimaced instead. "That damn place. After that night, after all these years, I don't know whether it was good or bad. Maybe a little of both." His body started to shake and he lowered his head.

A chill ran up my spine. The room suddenly seemed oversized, overwhelming. "Detective Wallis?" My words sounded far off and strange, the pleading words of a frightened kid.

The old man's head snapped up, fixing me in a haunted stare. *"Do you still see things up here?"*

As much as I tried with all my might, I couldn't help going limp, falling back into the chair. "No," I heard myself say. "Not after that night." *How did he know?*

"I dedicated my life to uncovering secrets. This town, you know—" he waved a hand before returning it to fidget with the other hand—"is full of 'em. Secret alcoholics, secret wife-beaters and drug addicts—don't get me started. I think secrets are hardest on those who keep them. It's no different for anyone. Not even for me."

"Detective Wallis," I said, leaning forward. "What did you see?"

"I knew when I saw all of you that night," he continued, not hearing me. "But who was I going to tell? Who *could* I ever tell? I knew what I knew and did my job, filed the report and tried to forget the whole thing."

"What did you see?"

"I've always liked to go fishing. Do you like to fish?" he asked without waiting for me to answer. "I do a lot of fishing these days. Great way to relax, to think. Went fishing on almost every day off I had when I was working. Two weeks before what happened, I was at the pond up by your uncle's house—sorry, *your* house—hoping to catch some catfish, doing some night fishing. Around eleven o'clock, I packed up and was driving past the mine when I heard gunshots…"

As he spoke, the old man's words left me reeling. He stopped his car, following the sound of the shots coming from inside the mine….

"…there was a group of kids animated, agitated, gathered around someone on the ground, obviously hurt. I hollered at them, but they didn't hear me, just kept going, like a movie. When I started to go up to them, I almost fell into a hole between us, and fell back. I dropped my flashlight and it went out. I grabbed the Zippo from my shirt pocket and flicked it on."

What he saw in the flickering light wasn't human. It stretched out from every direction. In the center of the thing, was a boy offering him a pistol "Take it, please get it off me." An instant later, the Zippo went out.

"I scrambled forward and got to my feet, flicking that Zippo for dear life. It came on again and I saw a man lunging at me, screaming something like *"No open flames!"* I braced for us to connect but he passed right through me and I ran like nobody's business the hell out of there."

Everyone sees something different.

"You saw the future." I stood up. *"My God, you saw the future."*

Rick Wallis took a deep breath and sighed, as if releasing a long-held weight. Hands on his knees, he braced himself as he pushed from the chair. "What about you? That night, did you find what you were looking for?"

I didn't know how to answer his question. How to reconcile the past with whatever was to come? "That night," I said, "yes, I did."

He reached out and patted my arm. "It's getting late, Dr. Baker, I should go now."

"Thank you for coming, Detective Wallis."

"Thank you, *kid*."

I walked him to the front door, watching him as he shuffled toward his car. "Did you ever see anything else?"

The old man stopped. He turned back to me. "I'll tell you this, young man, I'm not afraid of dying. There's more to life than just living." He winked. "And a lot more after that."

I couldn't disagree. We exchanged smiles and I closed the door.

The night had come to an end.

———————

The next evening, with the Little Italy Festival in full swing, we came down Crumpton Hill into Harris. There was Bill and David, his husband Chris, Eve, Cami and her family, me and Casey and our sons. All gathered on Main Street as night fell. We piled together onto the tractor ride, the night wind blowing over our faces as the John Deere rolled through town. The tractor's roaring engine mingled with our triumphant shouts as we raised our arms to holler at passers-by moving down the sidewalk. Every person waved back, returning our wild cheers with friendly shouts as we passed. At the Wine Garden, a band I wasn't familiar with was playing. They sounded pretty good.

———————

Our lives went back to normal following Rayven's memorial over that Labor Day Weekend. For Casey, there were classes to teach, lectures to give and papers to grade. For me, clients to see. For both of us, Vince and John to love and raise as they grew much too fast. Before we knew it, they would be charting their own courses as independent people.

In early November, we received a small Priority Mail package from Eve. It contained Rayven's hotshot dog tags, recovered from the site where he and two other hotshots died. The pieces of tin, warped from the intense heat of the wildfire, were all that remained of my cousin

210

and best friend. Included with the dog tags was a handwritten note on a jagged piece of yellow paper torn from a legal pad.

Cousin
These belong at the house.
Evie

Rayven's dog tags hang from the branch of a strong and ancient tree deep in the woods. A quiet and private spot. Depending on the time of day, it is a place bathed in sunlight and shadow.

On warm nights, Casey and I lay together on the grass while our boys dash over the yard, chasing fireflies in the moonlight. Their laughter is haunting, reminding us of our own youth.

Universe, time, and meaning.

At such times I can feel a vast presence gathered just beyond the light. I hear their familiar voices call to me from the darkness of the tree line. Sometimes, I glimpse their shimmering faces, waiting.

When I look up into the night sky, their distant memories fall over me like rain above Uncle Vincent's house.

About the Author

Steven Beai is the author of the novel WIDOW'S WALK, the four-issue miniseries comic book, SPIFFINGTON, P.I., the acclaimed study of censorship in the entertainment industry, CENSORING THE CENSORS and over 200 short stories and articles appearing in numerous online and print publications. A Bram Stoker Award finalist, his work has been recognized in *Year's Best Fantasy and Horror*. He has served on the Executive Boards of both the Horror Writers Association and the Small Press Writers and Artists Organization. He lives in southern Colorado.

Curious about other Crossroad Press books? Stop by our website:
http://crossroadpress.com
We offer quality writing
in digital, audio, and print formats.

Subscribe to our newsletter on the website homepage and receive a
free eBook.